I0639558

LIZARD
LIES
DREAMING

A work of fiction by
Stacy R. Vanderwoude

For information about permission to reproduce selections from this book, write to Permissions, Hive Press,
8351 Crestwood Avenue, Munster, In. 46321

Book cover design by Edward Ashmont

Library of Congress Cataloging-in-Publication Data
Vanderwoude, Stacy
Lizard Lies Dreaming / Stacy Vanderwoude

ISBN 978-0-9708695-8-6

First Edition

Thank you.....

Georgeann Tonkovich
Charles Gramps Starrett
Beth Barno
Ken Withrow
Ed Ashmont

And to all the Muses I can not name.

∞

Charles Hactor

7th Journal

June 4, Friday 3:30pm

Dead mice and moldy spiders. How's that for an opening entry? That would be the taste sensation I had swimming in my mouth this morning when I woke up.

It's interesting how taste can bring up a memory, dredging up bits of feeling that my brain should have purged a long time ago. Glimpses of things probably better left alone.

This particular flavor reminds me of the drainage ditch here by Gram's house and the first summer I stayed with her. It wasn't much of anything, still isn't, just a trickle of brown stanky suds conveniently located a couple blocks from her place. Over the course of the summer that ditch had become a hide out for me, quiet and forgot about. No kids with patched up forts, no people walking their dogs. No one but me and some anemic trees that lined the banks.

Anyway, I should get to the point.

I remember this one day I went down to the ditch.

That's kind of an understatement. I remember this day because I can never forget it. This is no unburied bit of treasured memory. It's not pleasant in any way. It always comes back like halos before the migraine.

Get to the point.

Ok, here's the memory: I'm busting out the front door and into the furnace outside. Stepping into the street, I can see silvered reflections slithering up from the soft asphalt as I squint my eyes to the kamikaze gnats that dive- bomb me. I feel the sweat cascade from my face, down my back. I keep walking block after excruciating block until finally making it to the oasis of its banks, to the anemic trees, to the steep decline of dried up sludge. It hadn't rained much that year, everything had evaporated or disintegrated and the ditch was no exception. Its banks had baked into a crusty shell and its water had been reduced to a thread of sudsy sparkle.

I walk around for a while throwing rocks, chucking sticks into the water, until I catch something ripe on the stale air. Something rank like a sewer, something lush with decay. I look around on the ground and there it is, a lump of something not quite right, laying just a few inches shy of the ribbon of water. I walk closer.

And here I find death on the banks of my ditch, celebrating with the confetti of a thousand flies, decked out with a hero's cloak of graying sludge. A beached carp of untold proportions and he's staring up at me with deflated balloons of rotten jelly waiting for me to find him.

Waiting? Hero? Whatever.

Anyway, I'm fascinated to say the least. So I walk even closer.

Then that's when the joke's on me, and the full extent of its fragrance hits me like a Mack truck. I feel dizzy then nauseous as an oily feeling pervades my nostrils, moving it's way down, coating the back of my throat thick with pure evil.

I start to back away and through tear choked eyes I swear I see it grin, smiling up at me through the cloud of its rot, happy at my disgust as I'm stumbling backwards and upwards, away from the runny scales and maggot engorged gills. Because I know something is there on the contaminated beach, jumping from the carp onto my shoulders, piggy backing me all the way home. Something chewing at my ear telling me that this is just the beginning.

I took it personally. I took a dead fish very personally. This was the splash of cold water before the tidal wave and I know sometimes I'm still drowning and I can't see the shore and I wake up from those nightmares and I can still hear her....

I get ahead of myself.

For a week I couldn't breathe without smelling greasy decomposition, days I couldn't eat without tasting carp death. A week that was heralded in by my fishy friend and that being the worst week ever of my entire life.

I don't want to write that down. Not yet.

Anyway, that spoiled taste of fish reminds me of this morning and then that links up to why I had that taste in my mouth in the first place… the dream that had me last night.

It started in a basement. I hate basements. I'm walking down this really long hallway and it's all cinderblock and white peeling paint. It's really cold and the light is too dim. I come to a room at the end of the hallway and I'm about to walk in but I stop. I freeze because there are thin, gleaming threads suspended from the walls and

6

the ceilings and bad things will happen if I go in, if I touch one of these…*webs*. Things are skittering along them and dark furry dots are moving inside the gauzy enclosures. I start to wonder why I'm here, where I have to go and I know it's beyond this place but then something happens. Something moves in front of me, won't let me through.

She.

Long, thin, wispy white hair, impossible segmented legs. A lipstick smeared gash on her bumpy face opening, spitting out mumbled things like mutilated words. Disjointed and lopsided *she* stands, a mess of legs and angles, painted slash moving violently, grinding out sounds that make my ears bleed.

I can't move. It's like I'm not really there but I'm shivering with the cold of the basement. I want to move, need to but nothing listens, and my arms feel like they weigh a thousand pounds. So cold, I have never been this cold before and it makes me heavier and I start to wonder if this is what death feels like.

I hear something. Wakes me up from this frozen moment. Wailing. From down the other hallway past the spider-*she*. I know who this is, the voice, the reasons why I have to get past her.

But that doesn't happen.

Then there's something foggy over my eyes, soft and sticky. Webs all over me and I can feel them skittering across my skin, into my clothes, in my hair. I open my mouth to breathe and that's when

they fill my mouth plugging it up. They taste like
mildew and dried blood….

I was choking when I woke up, the taste of the
spiders mingled with the familiar tang of panic
that coated my tongue.

I don't think I want to write anymore on this.
Something wants out of my head, I know. This has
happened before, little jagged splinters of
unwanted thoughts that demand to be seen and
heard. Then I'm left to make sense of it and
slowly forget again and…whatever.

I think I need a vacation.

June 5, Saturday 10:00 AM

I'm leaving tonight. I just told Gram and she was none too happy about it. She lectured me about Louisiana being dangerous and stuff, you know the usual, "Charles, I really don't think you thought this through…" yeah I know she would rather me never to go back there ever again but….

I called Butch at the store too, told him I was taking a month off, and he told me to find a new job. Ok, things look pretty much wrapped up here.

This is nuts, I know, taking off like this but it's something I know I have to do. The dream last night clenched it.

I'm in that basement again, with the spiders and the *she*, but there's no sound, like the volume has been turned off. It's still cold as hell and I can barely move and I'm staring at the spider-*she*, trying to figure out how I'm gonna get past her without being sucked dry like a fly.

I remember why I'm here this time. The reason comes to me fast and clean. I have to get past this and get to her, stop her pain. With all the effort I can muster, I tell my legs to move and I inch my way closer to the *she*.

I prepare myself for the worst, but it doesn't come. Instead *she* slowly moves away, sweeping all the webs along with her, waiting for me to pass through.

Then my body feels warm again and I'm moving fast past her and down a hall, gliding like a ghost. It seems so long, miles and miles of dingy concrete walls passing without a sound. Then I'm standing in front of a white metal door. I know what's behind it and I go to grab the knob but it's too cold and I jerk my hand away.

I start to panic because I need to get inside. I know she's behind that door. A sudden movement catches my eye down at the floor. There are fingers moving there, wiggling out from underneath the door like little white worms. I reach for them but they stop moving and turn too cold to ever be alive in the first place. I want to scream, but there's a pain in my chest, stabbing at my lungs and I fall on my side. The basement fades into suffocating black.

I hear something growl. It's so loud that I feel it in my bones, slowly realizing that the noise is thunder and I open my eyes to a blurry mess. From what I can tell I'm laying in mud, feeling the thick wet of it and that's when I hear the squeal of

pigs.

I go to stand and instead slip and fall on my

hands but when I look up I see something far off.

A figure standing in the same muddy field as me

but smudged out from recognition. I finally stand

up without falling and start to walk towards it and

I see it is a woman with dark, long hair and as

soon as I thought it, she starts to move away with

each step I take. Then I hear the squealing again

but now it comes from behind me.

I turn around too fast and slip into the muck

again. I'm afraid that the pigs are there but instead

my face turns to the mud and what's coming clean

with the rain. Floating in the dark slime are toes

and some are connected to a disconnected foot,

then a severed arm, and some fingers all

swimming together in the filth. All these things around me cut up and dead.

Then I wake up.

The stinging stench of pig shit hung heavy in the dark of my room, tricking me into thinking I was back home in Louisiana. It was the pig farm down the road from us, the way it would smell after a heavy rain. Laying in bed listening to the thunder, the pungent scent of the hogs drifting in with the moist air. It took a second for me to realize that *that* shouldn't be possible. I flipped on the light and instantly the smell disappeared with the darkness. I thought I was awake, maybe not. This is what has been freaking me out. These dreams have been so much more than what I normally experience, more coherent and real. It's hard to be sure where I'm at when I wake up.

My thoughts keep going back to the figure

standing in the mud, the blurry girl that wouldn't

let me see.

June 7, Monday 11:15 PM

Took me a little longer to get here than I expected. Bad tire in southern Indiana. Found a motel outside Baton Rouge.

The place is pretty seedy but quiet and cheap. I gave the weird guy at the desk $150.00 for five nights. My money's not gonna last long, I'll have to find cash somewhere soon.

I can't believe I made it! Louisiana doesn't seem familiar to me though. Probably been too long. I think Clearwater is still ten or twenty miles away. I'll just set up camp here for a while, take my time. Goodnight.

June 8, Tuesday 10:20 AM

This morning I was getting the rest of my gear from the car and this sketchy little guy, who turned out to be the motel owner, came up to me and asked if I was an artist, well, a painter to be exact. "You got all those brushes and goofy stuff, you know."

He's short and skinny, dark hair, weird eyes. He said his name is Gristoff. Then he started to ask me where I was from, what I was doing here. I decided to lie and tell him I was on my way to New Orleans, stopping here to take in the local scenery. It sounded lame but it worked, he stopped with the questions. Except for one.

"Would you be interested in making a few bucks?"

I closed the trunk of the car and turned around, "Doing what?"

I followed him to his cramped little office where he wrote out some numbers on a ketchup- smeared napkin. It was an address of a warehouse in town, some guy who needed someone to paint it. It's not commissioned portraits but hell I'll take it.

I went to thank him but he started to back away, not wanting to touch my outstretched hand, his eyes bulging out like a dead carp, knocking himself into a filling cabinet.

Strange fucker.

I'm off to the warehouse.

June 8, Tuesday 11:30 PM

Just got back from my new place of

employment....

Not so bad, I guess. I'm painting a whole

warehouse electric blue. Interesting color choice, I

can handle it.

Anyway, I met the owner of this warehouse. His

name is Slather, pocked marked face and sandy

thin hair. Nervous, always looking around, wonder

why.

The other guy I'm painting with is Tim. He's

cool, my age, from the next town over.

Tim says Slather's a dealer. Slather told me he

just stores auto parts. Go figure. Tim also told me

that Slather could pretty much get anything you'd

want so I mentioned maybe placing an order for some Xanax.

"Trouble sleeping or something?"

"Yeah Tim, you could say something like that."

June 10, Thursday 7:46pm

Way too fucking hot to paint.

Second thoughts about the job? Yeah, I guess I

could say that.

The asshole screams at us all day, whenever we

try to take a break, get some shade, get a drink,

whatever, he's there like a bad rash yelling about

getting it done, get back out there, no breaks, fuck

you.

Well, I'm done for the day. Tim broke out some

skunk before I left, calmed the nerves a little. He

asked me about where I was from, why I was here,

shit like that. I said that I was from Chicago,

taking a vacation, going to New Orleans, trying to

make some money on the way.

But nothing about why I'm really here. Sometimes I want to spill it, ask for help, advice, anything. I never do though.

O.K. now to the interesting part, this dream I had last night. I've been thinking on it all day and it doesn't fade, all the parts still there in detail. This has to be something, don't quite know what. The intensity was incredible.

I was trapped inside something tight, wet. The walls were slick, and my fingers stretched through where I touched it. It felt like skin.

I noticed that it was getting hot and I started to panic, gulping in heated air, wanting to be out of this. Too constrained, too close, I was tearing at the fleshy walls, fingers gouging into thick softness and it started to rip. More hot air rushed in but it was dry and it stung my eyes as I scrambled out, falling onto something like sand, melding with my sweat, grit coated my skin. I looked up to see someone standing above me but the figure was so blurry I couldn't tell who it could be.

Then I felt something on my face soft and cool, smooth hands holding my head up.

Then I heard the blur speak, "Come into this circle. Breathe your name wide."

These words were female, low, and soft. Instantly it soothed my panic and I tried to open my eyes again, tried to see who was speaking to me. I could make out a round face, long, dark hair, and a faint smell of flowers that rode the burn of the air. My lack of sight smudged out any true detail from her face and this overwhelming rush of regret exploded in my chest.

"Please let me see you," my voice cracked with the want of it, I needed to.

Then her touch wasn't cool anymore. Instead it turned warm, then hot and it stung like sunburn. The soft smear of her face was changing hue, the brightness of the desert being replaced with pink light, vivid like rare meat. I felt my heart squeeze itself into a tight fist, breath lodged and stuck, caught in my closing throat. The pink glow focused around her shoulders, constricting, turning darker, forming into a bloody halo above her head.

I was kneeling in the sand, I couldn't move. Wouldn't. I would not leave her, even though the panic ran through me like electric and my chest was about to explode. I was going to stay here until I saw her. Something so important....

Her scorching fingers ran through my hair, to the back of my head. Her touch was incredible, every hair on my body stood on end. The sweetness of the flowers was closer, stronger but not overpowering. Then there was hot breath on my lips, in my mouth, taking it into my starving lungs. She was so close, so much closer to me and I could feel the swell of lips brush against mine. My mouth watered but I couldn't swallow, my body one giant throb of pain but I couldn't move. Closer, come on, closer. Incredible pressure on my lips, then fire in between as she spread my mouth apart.

I waited for the taste of her but it never came. That's when I woke up mummified in the wet sheets, the smell of desert and fading flowers still drifting inside my brain. Incredible. These dreams are getting so insane.

I can close my eyes and still hear that voice, feel it vibrate in my ears, whispery and smooth like warm honey inside my head, coating everything thick. I couldn't stop thinking about this if I wanted to. And I don't want to.

I've got to sleep. Maybe she'll come back tonight.

June 13, Sunday 8:33 PM

It's been two days since I've been to the warehouse, because it's taken that long to get my shit together. No cops have been around asking questions, so I'm thinking it's been taken care of or something like that. I hope.

Here goes...

I went to work as usual on Friday, still way too hot to paint. Around eleven I went into the warehouse to get some shade. That's when I saw Slather. He was a million times more nervous than usual and he had a couple of these huge gorillas with him. He kept barking orders about not letting anyone in and keeping an eye out for anybody coming to the doors. Kept repeating it, he was really freaked.

Slather saw me come in and shook his head, "Hey Picasso, get the fuck outside and paint, that's what I'm fucking paying you for. Understand? Out!" and shoved me towards the door. He smelled bad, an old crusty sweat stench mixed with his crappy breath.

I went back outside. That's when I saw Tim leaning up against the blue of the warehouse, looking none too good. He'd been at my place the night before with a couple bottles of Jack. He left with half a bottle around three in the morning.

"Do you mind if I take off, man?"

I got a headache just looking at him. So he left and I stayed and painted.

It was around one thirty when Slather's two monkeys came outside. They stood some ways from my ladder, lighting up their smokes.

"I could use a beer."

"Yeah, they're half price at Gino's during lunch. Let's go."

" I doubt anyone is showing up today anyway."

"That's because no one is ever going to show up. The fuck's paranoid, thinks everyone's out to get him. Come on, he won't even know we're gone. He swallowed enough pills to knock out a rhino for Christ's sake."

They flicked their cigarettes to the ground and started to walk to an old shitty looking Caprice. By the third try it started up. They laughed at me as they drove past.

My thoughts drifted to Slather. I bet he wouldn't know I was gone either. Who was he so scared of? Who was out to get him? I'm sure a lot of people were. I knew I didn't want to get involved in this, so I started to pack up my stuff.

Then I heard a car coming closer. It didn't sound like the Caprice, didn't think the gorillas would be back so soon. Couple seconds later a black vintage Jag pulled up beside my ladder.

Crap.

The door opened and that's when he got out. Dressed in black, just like his Jag. Nice suit, tailored, looked expensive. He glanced up at me.

I should have said something, anything but I couldn't. Not when I saw this guys eyes. Green. Way too green. Something bothered me, it seemed wrong. I couldn't just chalk it up to colored contact lenses, something gave me the chills about the way he looked at me.

He broke away to duck inside the car. He brought out a doctors bag and slung it on the roof with a thud. He smiled and turned, heading for the side door of the warehouse.

A doctor? Maybe Slather called him.

I stood on the ladder for a couple of minutes, listening to the birds, feeling the sun on my face. Everything seemed in slow motion, suspended. Then a different noise split the moment, a loud crash coming from inside the warehouse.

The Voice of Reason inside my head was giving me detailed directions to my hotel room as I started to climb down the rungs, paintbrush in hand. I stopped to listen. Nothing. I snuck up to the warehouse door. Listened. Nothing. What the hell was going on in there?

Maybe it was nothing.

So what was I doing standing at the door? I needed to see. I always need to see, so I opened it. Inside was dark and cool as I walked in. Now, I knew Reason wasn't too happy about this because there were no good reasons to be found for me going in. I hadn't really thought this out, I mean, what the hell was I going to do if there was something going on?

My eyes adjusted and I could see Slather's office door was open about half way. I could hear noises, a grunt, heavy things being dragged then dropped.

Then a giggle, quiet and weird.

I crept closer and hid behind a crate, trying to get a gist for what was happening behind the half open door. I could see a table to the extreme left and on it was the doctor's bag, a brown glass

bottle, and a bunched up rag.

I moved over to the left and caught the figure of

the green- eyed man bent over something. Then he

stepped to the right and out of my view and that's

when I saw Slather lying face up on the desk,

naked and unconscious, arms tied down to the

metal legs, beyond that I couldn't see anything

past his stomach.

That's when I should have run. Because at any

minute he could have come out of that room to

find me there behind that crate, but instead I

noticed Slather's head beginning to move and his

eyes started to open.

Green eyes stepped into view again, his back

towards me. He stood there watching him, waiting

for him to totally wake up. Then Slather slurs out some sounds, then a solid word.

"Wait…"

Green eyes was now heading for the nifty leather bag that was sitting on the table. Slowly he opened it and began to take out shiny silver things, laying them neatly in a row.

"What? Wait a minute…"

He came around to Slather's left side and looked down. I could see his face then, on it a smile growing wider, and I could hear Reason advising me not to look at his eyes.

"Razor?"

Razor?

In latex sheathed hands he held something like a pair of scissors and made a cutting gesture in front of Slather's panicked face. Then the instrument touched his bare chest, the tip making its way to his right nipple. Then stopped.

"What the…" Cut short by the snip. Slather started to scream as the blood filled in the hole where his nipple used to be. Razor laughed as he wiped his scissors clean.

"Fuck me! No more! Let me up! Let me up!" Slather screamed, slamming his head against the desk. But Green eyes had already walked back to the table, picking up another instrument, a long one, skinny with a blade at the tip.

"What did I do, Razor? What the fuck did I ever do to you?" Now he was gasping, his face red with tears, voice high with anxiety.

Razor was back at his side again, smile gone, eyes narrowed into slits. "I remember when I had to do the emergency appendectomy on you." His voice low, dangerous, "Had to anesthetize you with ether because that's all I had to work with. But it did get the job done." He was examining Slather's torso, "Yes, right here. I closed you up nice." His hand pressed on the scar.

"Real nice," said with a growl, the low calm of his voice seemed swallowed up into the depths of that hellish green.

"Is all of this about the morphine? I... I didn't take it. Hey man, it was Johnston not me. Hey, Razor, wait..." Right then Razor's left hand that was holding the scalpel made a quick movement downwards, laying open the area of skin. His smile was growing wider and wider.

And Slather screamed and screamed.

I was shaking, my stomach making weird heaving movements. I was frozen in place. How the hell was this happening?

"Oh stop it, I just cut the skin, I'm not even down to the muscle yet!" His right hand shiny red, pressed down on the slit as he made the movement again, turning it into a gaping hole.

Then the screaming stopped. Blood was coming thick and fast down the side of his body, dripping off the desk, and pooling on the concrete floor. Slather had passed out.

Green eyes slapped his pasty face, "None of that…you can sleep when you're dead," Slather's eyes fluttered, rolling up into his head, "Let's go! Wake up!" Awake, Slather made some kind of horrid retching noise that was then followed by an eruption of puke.

"That was unpleasant. Back to your question, you asked me what you ever did to me," his words cold and short, "Well, it's not about what you did to me, its what you did to *her*."

A new look of horror appeared on Slather's face.

Razor bent down close, "You're a piece of shit, Slather. Always have been. Gila may forgive you but I never will and I've waited so long to do this." That's when Slather started to squirm like a fish out of water, pushing more of his dwindling blood onto the reddening floor.

"Oh my," he smirked. "That's a lot of blood you're losing." He bent down closer, "But I'm not going to watch you bleed to death," his words seethed through his grinding teeth, " That would take entirely too long and I just don't have the patience these days." His hand ran down Slather's chest, across the absent nipple, down to the gaping

gash of his reopened scar, and that's where his

fingers slid into, disappearing deep inside the

incision.

Slather drew in a sharp gasp and then let out the

worst scream yet. He screamed without taking a

breath because it seemed air wasn't important

anymore, his pain was all-consuming. Blood was

gushing like water from a faucet. Slippery crimson

coated Razor's arm as he jerked up and then out of

the opening, flinging more blood and bits of

Slather onto the wall.

A piece flew through the open door and landed

with a splat next to the crate I was hiding behind.

It was thick and dark red, and something nested in

the center, slimy and gleaming.

The vomit was already coming out my nose before I could think about it and I felt myself folding into a pathetic mass of jelly right there on the warehouse floor. I tried to steady myself, took a deep breath and listened. Everything was quiet. He must have been dead or close to it.

As I write this I ask myself if I felt pity at that moment. Did I want to jump up and help Slather? Now that he was dead, did I feel some kind of remorse for not doing anything? I really don't think I did. That bothers me, I mean am I some kind of monster? Or did he choose this? Was this a predictable outcome to his chosen line of work? He must have done something pretty bad to piss off that Razor doctor guy, right? Or am I part of the problem for being so callous, for not really giving a shit?

Back to the story, I was still on my knees, listening for any kind of noise when I looked up to see a blur of black coming towards me. Fight or flight finally kicked in as I tried to scramble away from Dr. Psychotic and his shiny black leather bag full of delights. But before I could get anywhere, he reached down and grabbed my arm, jerking me up from the floor. I looked into his face and saw no trace of that lunacy hiding in his gaze. What I did see was a strange look of concern.

"You O.K.?" Yeah, that's what he said.

I nodded like an idiot as I looked into his eyes. Reason was screaming at me not to do that but I did and I started to feel an ache in my temples, turning to a slight burn. I tried to close my eyes, but they wouldn't. I felt stuck, like a special K trip, my jaw clenched shut, I couldn't move. Then the sensation turned to a blinding stab, like a hot butter knife through my skull. But through this all I could hear a whisper, "Will you tell?" It was so clear, like it was coming from *inside* my head and I could swear his lips never moved.

Will I tell? NO! The answer screamed out in my head. I didn't want any of this. I wasn't about to tell anyone, I wanted to walk away. This was none of my business.

Then the pain was gone and he looked away, a small smile on his face. He patted me on the arm and reached inside his shirt pocket to pull out a card. "Here, it's an address for another job, if you want it. I think your tenure here is pretty much through." His smile faded and that dark in his green flashed sharp, "Tell them Razor sent you." He turned away to walk back into the blood soaked office and I could hear the brisk snap of

latex gloves.

What should I do? I think I should go, the job at

the warehouse is over, and he was nice enough not

to kill me. Anyway I don't think I could stay

away, this little vacation keeps getting more and

more interesting.

June 14, Monday 6:20 PM

I just got back from my new place of
employment. After popping a trank, I was ready to
follow through on the deal Razor offered.

The place was hard to find. I tried to ask for
directions in town but anyone I talked to suddenly
seemed not to speak English and would look at me
in this weird spacey way. I wasn't sure if it was a
question of genetics or they couldn't believe I
really wanted to know where the place actually
was.

I finally found it along an old decrepit gravel
road. It was a huge plantation home, complete
with looming, weepy trees, and tall white pillars.
Oh yeah, and a huge, old, white Caddy was parked
in the front.

I walked up to the door and whacked the iron

gargoyle knocker. I was nervous. What the hell

was I thinking?

The door swung open and I was confronted by

the incomprehensible girth of a monstrous brotha.

He just stood there and starred at me, probably

expecting an apology for wasting his time.

"Razor sent me."

I offered the damp, crumpled card. He looked

down at it and stepped to the side, opening the

door a little wider, "Follow me."

The foyer of the house was huge and dark. The

air smelled like moldy wool and it was much

hotter inside than out. To the right were two

French doors, firmly shut. To my left was a dining

room, painted a deep blood red with black

lacquered chairs and a huge rectangular table. In

front of me was a shadowy staircase, which I was being led to. I looked up and I could see at least two more floors. We stopped at the second, made a quick right, and walked through an open door.

I found myself standing in a very white room. White carpet, white glossy walls, white desk with a really big, fat guy with pasty white skin dressed in a really big white suit sitting behind it. The one who led me up the stairs went up to the desk and whispered a few things to him and then left the room without a glance.

He was staring at me. I started to sweat more, could feel it running down my back. What the hell was I getting myself into?

The man's head was huge, his face seemed out of place in comparison to his cranium, the features too small, making him look all the more devious. Then he tried to form a smile.

"What do they call you, son?"

What do they call me? I don't know I'm too busy staring at your head. "Um, Charlie, Charlie Hactor."

"Very good, please sit, Charlie," his voice thick and intrusive.

The chair that I sat in was white vinyl and it instantly stuck to my sweaty legs. Now it was his turn to eyeball me. I looked away, I didn't want to be rude, staring at his head and all, instead I glanced up at the wall behind him, and saw shelves with nothing on them, walls with no pictures at all, just all white.

"So, Razor recommends you?"

Suddenly my head hurt, that dull pain stabbed at my brain again. I could hear those words, 'Will you tell?'.

I couldn't remember what he just asked me, my thoughts were all over the place. Wait, Razor, recommending me. I nodded.

"I need an artist. I need a mural painted of my family. It will be on the wall of the downstairs hall. So, does this sound like something you would be interested in, Charlie?"

I couldn't believe this. "Yeah, very much so, but don't you need to see any of my work?"

"No, I think you will do just fine. Now let's show you where you'll be working."

He rose from the desk with surprising ease. His bulk was impressive, he was almost perfectly round, like a beach ball wrapped in an expensive suit.

We made it downstairs, past the dining room to a long hallway that connected to what looked like the kitchen.

"You can come as early as you wish, work all day, leave at dark. I conduct business then. I'll pay a hundred a day to start off with. This may change with your progress," he mopped at his gleaming forehead, "You can walk the grounds and explore the rooms that aren't locked. Talk to the family members that are here, they may give you some insight to what you need to paint. Don't worry you will have an outline of the various family that I will want painted. You may desire some more information on them, is all I'm saying, to flesh them out, so to speak."

There was something way to good to be true about this, Reason whispered in my head. I told it to shut up.

He turned to look me square in the face, "I'm hoping you will become like family to us. I think you will fit in just fine." His eyes hardened at that little comment and at the same time he held out his puffy mitt of a hand. I shook it really not wanting to.

"Splendid!" said with thunderous laughter and with that he waddled away, leaving a strung-out looking guy with blonde hair standing in his place.

"New guy?"

"Yeah."

"I'm Splint. That was Johnston," he glanced over his shoulder, "don't fuck with him or with me, for that matter."

His eyes were cashed, red, and watery. I started to notice a pungent aroma creeping in from where he stood.

"Where you from?"

"Chicago."

"Hmm. So, what do you want to know?" Looking back over his shoulder again.

"Well, what do you guys do around here?" Maybe I shouldn't have asked that one. Splint turned, his watery gaze drying up into a hard and mean stare, looking me square in the eye. He smiled, but it was wrong. A guy like that should never smile.

"All kinds of stuff, Charlie boy." Letting out a quiet, stained laugh. "We do all kinds of fun stuff here."

His scare tactics bounced off my growing Xanax

buzz. I just wanted to know what actually

happened around there, and what he meant by

stuff.

He started to walk away so I followed. We

reached the kitchen, all stainless steel, shiny and

new looking.

"This is the kitchen."

Thanks for the update. We backtracked into the

dinning room, into the foyer, and back

up the stairs. I saw that Johnston's office door was

shut.

"Johnston's office," he pointed a finger at the

closed door. "Don't go in there." We walked past

a couple more rooms, "My room, Mother's old

room, and Slather's."

A jolt went through me. Slather's? This made no sense, Razor recommends me but kills him and he lived here? Did they know he was even dead? Reason made the suggestion to keep my mouth shut. I agreed.

"Who's Mother?" Trying to get my mind off of it.

Splint kept walking, "Johnston's. The old bat finally bought the farm."

We were now at the end of the hall. To my right was a little alcove holding a thin flight of stairs leading up.

"Third floor. Used to be Lucretia and Delilah's room. Toulmac's before he moved into the basement with Mother. That was a long time ago." He stood in front of the stairs, his eyes far away.

"Who were they?"

His eyes snapped back on mine, "Family long gone. Nothing up there now." He squeezed past me, making his way back down the hall.

"Does the Doc stay here too?"

Splint stopped dead in his tracks. I could see his shoulders creep up into his neck. "How do you know about him?"

"He's the one who told me about this gig. So is he like the family doctor or something?"

"Johnston's doctor," he said quietly and he turned. I could see something there on his face, fear? Anger? His eyes were dark and sketchy. "He stays upstairs." He looked back up the alcove, "I wouldn't go up there if I were you."

From there, we went back downstairs and out the front door, around the side of the house into the back yard. I don't think 'backyard' is the right word here. Maybe gardens would be better, very lush and many, many flowers.

I noticed that Splint looked worse out in the sun. His skin had a nasty yellow tinge to it and a bluish bag hung under each squinty eye.

The garden seemed to go pretty far back and I really wanted to walk it but Splint had other ideas. "This is the yard. O.K., this tour is over."

Just then, I saw someone moving, coming through some bushes. A blue bandana attached to a heavily wrinkled face, her eyes caught mine. She smiled and waved.

"Hey, who's that?"

"I don't see anybody." Splint looked annoyed.

I looked back and she was gone. "She was an old black lady, blue bandana on her head. Didn't you see her?"

He didn't answer, just kept walking.

When we got back to the house, he handed me an envelope. "Here, this is your sign on bonus. Make sure to be here tomorrow, bright and shiny. Got it?"

I took the envelope and glanced to my right, a flood of green distracted me from the weight of cash in my hand. The French doors connected to the foyer were open now, so I decided to take a peek.

Green. Everything green. Walls, carpet, drapes. I took a step closer through the doors. The room was narrow, long and huge, and way, way back in the corner was a stage draped with green velvet.

I felt a tap on my shoulder.

"I'll show you that when you're ready," he breathed into my ear. Reason said it was time to go.

I spun around to catch the lopsided opening of his mouth stretching itself up into that grin, an imposter of a smile. Chills broke through my numbed nerves and goose bumps covered my arms even in the thick humid heat of the foyer.

He walked slowly to the door and opened it, signaling me to leave.

So I did, gladly.

What to think? Should I go through with it? There's so much to think about. I also have to keep my perspective on why I came here in the first place. But there's something there, something about the place that itches.

I need to know more about the Doc, and about

all the *stuff* that goes on there.

June 15, Tuesday 10:22 PM

I got to the Johnston household early, around
7:30, found brushes and a few opened cans of
paint in the hallway. I primed the walls and waited
for them to dry and then added another coat. The
house was pretty quiet. I guess no one was home.

I sat on the porch and sketched some ideas for
Johnston, made a list of things I needed, ate my
lunch and put another coat of primer on the walls.

I left around 3:00 and drove around town
looking for a home improvement place, paint
store, anything. Finally found a hardware store
where I bought the paint and brushes I needed,
pretty much using up the $150.00 bonus I got from
Splint yesterday.

I thought about looking for Tim, but decided not to, so I went back to the hotel. I didn't feel like explaining all the crazy shit that's happened since Slather's tragic episode.

I took another trank and stretched out on the lumpy mattress. I didn't even feel myself falling asleep.

I was hot again, and it was dark. I heard a murmuring like a low hum of chanted sounds and suddenly the dark opened up to desert light. I walked on the sand, the grains pushing warm between my toes. The sun was strong and I felt it on my shoulders, dry and heavy. I was hearing the muffled voice becoming clearer, the rumble turning into structured words, into the deep huskiness of her voice.

"It will be all right."

Whispered now but hearing it clearly. I walked towards her voice, over a low hill of rock and that's where I saw them.

"I will take the sun for you."

She sat on the ground, the source of the sound, the woman standing in the mud, the sexy voice telling me to breathe my name wide. Long, black hair. Bronzed, smooth skin. Sweat flooded her pretty rounded face, making her high cheeks shine and her full lips gleam. The same lips that pushed against mine.

"Razor, I will take your water."

That's when I noticed what she held in her arms, laying in her lap.

Lucky bastard.

He looked dead, his face red with the heat, half naked, limp and lifeless. Brown arms held him tight, her golden skin clashed with his pale flesh. He jerked, twitched. She held tighter.

"This will be over soon."

She was shaking small, violent shivers, teeth clattering, muscles clenching. She gathered him up closer, holding on for dear life it seemed.

Razor's arm jerked up and grabbed onto her shoulder and that's when I saw the marks on his pink skin. Lines, jagged gouges, raised and angry. There were scars all over his arms, a few on his chest. Some looked old, faded, some scabbed and fresh.

"Sleep now, peyote will be done with you soon."

The light was growing fainter, the heat disappearing. Soft, softer, darker then dark.

Significance? Couldn't say, but it does stand strong in my mind. This one is like the others, too realistic and coherent to shrug off, to say it was

only a dream.

June 17, Thursday 3:00AM

I can't sleep, don't want to, couldn't if I did. Crazy shit tonight, I should say last night. Doesn't matter. Insane stuff, can't believe it, got to calm down, get it together. Start at the beginning.

Hold on, let me light this smoke, O.K. ... here we go.

When I made it to work today, the house seemed deserted again. My envelope was in the hallway, the hundred bucks promised. I decided to walk around, see what I could see. I went upstairs. Johnston's door was shut and locked but then I tried the next one. Splint's. It opened.

The first thing that hit me was the smell, old sweat layered with the sour tang of mildew. I turned on the light, total chaos. Magazines

covered the floor. I picked up a bizarre one with a

bondage boy being fisted by a hairy fucker in a

leather suit, I threw it back on the pile. I noticed

the closet was opened a crack, so you know I had

to look in. I pulled the hanging silver chain and

instantly Splint's private library was revealed.

I was impressed that Splint could read. There

were no clothes taking up space on these shelves,

instead they sagged with the weight of family

favorites such as, *Hitler: A Life of Purity, The*

Third Reich Manifesto, Demonology Through the

Ages, it goes on and on.

A whole lot of material on the occult, Nazi

propaganda, bondage manuals, and some Crowley

stuff, but when I saw what was on the next shelf,

that's what creeped me out. Lined up were kids

books, coloring books, and comics of cartoon characters.

What the fuck was he doing with those? I pulled the chain.

I turned towards his bed and something hanging on the wall above it caught my eye, something long and black. I walked closer and saw that it was like a nightstick or a club and the wall behind it was smeared with dried blood, crusty and brown-red. This guy was really turning out to be quite the wanker.

I turned off his light and backed up into the hallway. I went for the next door, locked. I think that was Slather's. I wonder if they knew yet, or maybe Johnston had him greased, still none of my business.

I tried the last door and the knob turned. I was

starting to feel like Goldielocks.

This one was just right.

The light filtered in a weak golden color through

the old lace of the curtains that hung in the one

window. There was a strange smell to this room

but I couldn't put my finger on it, I think it

reminded me of my old biology teacher Mr.

Eddington. This space was decorated in that old

lady, doily sort of way; stripped wallpaper, crystal

lamps, knitted bedspread. I walked over to the

closet and the smell intensified when I opened it.

Inside were long black gowns hanging in thick

plastic, and old hat boxes lined the shelf above. I

was thinking about taking a couple of them down

but that stench was giving me a headache so I

closed the door.

My head was getting worse, the pounding making me queasy so I went to the window and opened it wide. The air rushed in hot but at least it smelled good and the fumes started to clear out. I was about to go back to the closet and snoop some more but I decided to sit down on the bed and give my brain a rest.

At that time it was probably 2:00 or 3:00 in the afternoon but when I woke up the room was dark. I fell asleep, how the hell did I manage that? The air was cooler and damp and the musty old bed cover was wrapped around me.

I realized with terror that it was dark and remembered what Johnston had told me about leaving at night. I also realized that I was hearing voices coming from the foyer and they were getting louder, making their way up the stairs. The door was shut, the lights off, no one comes in here, right? Jesus, I was thinking about climbing out the window when I heard thumps and muffled voices coming through the ceiling. They were above me now, on the third floor, why? There was nothing up there, right?

I sat still and listened, I got up and felt my way to the door and opened it.

I had two choices; go downstairs as quietly as I could, get into my car that I'm sure they all saw parked there and go back to my hotel room. Or see what they were doing. Right.

I reached the thin flight of stairs and the voices floated down as I started the climb up. The stairs creaked and I stopped, I was ready to book my ass downstairs but no one came down to shoot me, so I started again.

Third floor.

It was smaller than the second, almost like an attic. Through the wooden railing I could see a door slightly open and caught a glimpse of Johnston walking around something in the middle of the room. I crouched down on the third step, trying to see what the fuck they were doing without being spotted myself. Johnston stepped aside and that's when I saw what they were standing around. It was a bed and what I could see of it was two brass posts and a wadded up white sheet. Then a foot with a thin chain around it kicked out from behind the door. This was unbelievable.

Splint appeared at the foot of the bed, his eyes dark and freaked, chewing on his lip, hands jammed into his pockets.

"Hold her good boys. She bites." Johnston's voice drifted from somewhere in the room.

Then a hissing noise, a grunt and some curses, I could see Splint pacing the floor but I still couldn't see what they were doing.

"Goddamn it!" Someone shouted, and that's when the door banged open as a skinny guy flew through it and slammed into the railing just above my head. I squatted down on the stairs as quick as I could, praying he didn't see me. He got up, cracked his neck, and shuffled back inside.

Now the door was open all the way.

There were about five of them, all standing around the bed, holding someone down. Johnston was on one side, holding a syringe in his swollen hand, drawing something up and then tapping it with his finger.

"This is really Razor's job, but if I must…" he rumbled sounding irritated.

Two of the men moved aside to give Johnston better access and that's when I saw what was on the bed. *Who* was on the bed. My mind froze and Reason refused to see what I was trying to comprehend. It was *her*, the muddy figure, the peyote girl, the woman of my dreams, literally. Here she was, about to be sedated or even killed. Her face wasn't gleaming any more, no serene mannerisms, no dream-like poses instead it was tight with darkness, flushed with violence. Her eyes were black and insane, teeth barred and clenched shut and a strangled hissing was coming from in between.

I didn't know what to do. I felt like I should have done something but what? I was outnumbered, no doubt about that. My mind was racing with so much new information, and so many questions. None of this made any sense. How was she there on that bed in this house?

The skinny fuck that had been thrown from the room a little earlier was now holding off her arm waiting for Johnston to slide the needle in. It took him a few tries but finally the fat fucker found a vein. After a few minutes she quit hissing and after a couple more she quit moving. The group started to shuffle away from the bed.

There was a noise from downstairs. Crap. I climbed up the rest of the stairs and crawled my way to a grandfather clock that stood to the right of the door. I pressed myself into the wall, hoping that the shadows were deep enough to hide me.

There was pounding on the stairs, louder on the second floor, heavy breathing coming up to the third. He swung around the railing and I could see his face, that insane green of his eyes smoldering, his features like stone. I know he saw me in that corner, I could feel that stab in my head as he glanced over me but didn't stop. Instead he barged through the door and I lost sight of him. I wasn't about to move.

I heard a thud and a voice of one of Johnston's guys, "Hey, easy Doc."

"Well how good of you to come, Doctor," Johnston's thick words mocking.

"Get away from her." Very quietly said, I could barely hear it.

"Come on now, Razor. You know the agreement."

"Get the fuck away from her." Razor's voice was still calm but there was something there that made your hair stand on end. Bad things seem to happen when you piss off the Doc.

"Here, this is what I need from Gila. Tell her and we will leave." Johnston said, and I heard the crumple of paper, silence, then a faint murmur, a whisper, I couldn't make out the words.

"Good. It is done. The question proposed, let the prophet dream. We will leave her now."

Footsteps coming close to the door, they all started to file out from the room, past me and down the stairs. Splint was the last one to leave and it seemed he couldn't get out of there fast enough.

Her name was Gila. She is real. How was this possible?

I could hear voices deep from downstairs, I think from the green room. How was I going to get past them? Then I heard a slam and the voices faded away.

A part of me wanted to go into that room, ask what all of this meant. I wanted to look at her face, sit next to her on that bed, and maybe she would wake up and tell me that this is some freaky psychic thing shared between us, she was having dreams about me too. Tell me I'm not crazy, please. Then kiss me.

Maybe deep down this is what I really want. A connection, an acknowledgement. Get into my head and see what I see then I'll see what you see. Look at me with real eyes, put those lips on mine for real, experience their incredible burn. I will get into that bed with you, press myself into you, move up that smooth, warm skin because your

skin is my skin and I would be the one to open

your mouth and go inside.

Nice fantasy. I forgot about ole green eyes in

there with her. Who was he to her? Who the hell

was he? I can't think about this anymore. It hurts.

I wrote it down, now to sleep.

June 17, Thursday 5:30 Pm

I'm a little low on sleep, so I hope this makes sense.

I went to work around noon today, tried to sketch some more ideas on Johnston and Splint but last night's images kept poking through.

I wasn't alone this time, though. Splint was there, wasn't much for conversation but that was fine with me.

I really wasn't getting anything done so I thought about sneaking up to snoop on her. Splint finally went into the green room and closed the doors. I waited a few minutes before I headed up the stairs. Did I think I would see her? My heart was pounding while I took each step in slow motion, trying not to make the slightest noise.

I reached the second floor and again, Johnston's office door was closed. I made my way to the end of the hall. I noticed my shirt becoming heavy and I looked down to see it almost transparent with sweat. I started up the thin flight of stairs.

I wondered if she was still up there. Did she escape? Did Razor get her out in the early morning hours while everyone slept?

Last step, onto the third floor. Then something weird happened. The heat became different, the humidity was leaving, and the atmosphere seemed to become lighter. Then I started to smell something fresh and clean like clear desert air. I really couldn't think too much on it at that time. It seemed anything was possible as I stood there looking at the door I knew she was behind. What was I going to do? Should I knock? Go in? Would she try to kill me, not knowing who I was? What would Razor do? Was he in there?

I heard a groan on the stairs and I turned towards it and saw a face peering at me through the railings.

"Where you going, fuck head?"

Splint reached a hand through the wooden bars and hooked a finger at me, gesturing me to follow him.

So close.

We made it to Johnston's office, the humidity and heat a thousand times worse again. Splint glared into my face, "Don't go up there."

"Why?"

"Cause I said so. There's nothing up there."

"I saw someone up there."

Splint looked annoyingly surprised, "Really?"

"There was a woman up there." I had a bad feeling that Reason had left me for good.

Splint just stood there, searching my face for something, he looked confused. "She's no one."

"I…just…thought I'd put her in the mural, that's all."

"No, you won't. She's Johnston's business. Forget about her." His eyes were getting that weird, nervous look to them and he swallowed hard, "Don't go up there again."

I packed up and left after our little conversation. So she was Johnston's concern? I don't think I agree with that. I don't know exactly what she is or whose, but I'm going to learn more about her if they like it or not.

June 18, Friday 3:30 AM

I woke up about an hour ago. I know I won't get back to sleep, I'm out of Xanax.

I don't really want to write this down, I'd rather just forget about this one. Maybe I should go back home, to my Grandmother's. Reason keeps telling me there is where sanity is, in Chicago with her, safe and consistent.

Instead I'm making the choice to write it down, stay put, and think about it. I have a feeling that if I don't, I may never sleep again.

This dream was about Mom.

I don't know how to start, how to explain. This dream was mostly emotion, sharp and throbbing, like fresh pain from an old wound.

She was the one in pain, she was screaming with it, down in a basement. I tried to call out, I needed to find where she was, but I couldn't find her. Everything around me was dark, shadowy, and cloudy. I felt a huge weight of guilt like this was my fault, why she was down there in pain. Then I noticed that there was blood on the floor, I kept stepping in it and it was slippery and something was telling me it was hers.

Then I found myself standing in front of that familiar white metal door. I reached for the knob and my fingers felt the cooling warmth of blood covering it and a terrifying sense of urgency washed over my body. I opened the door.

I now stood in our living room in Louisiana and watched the scene I had imagined over and over again so long ago, a scene I never got to see. My

Mother was sitting at her small, wooden writing desk with the note in her hand, bleeding all over it, dying right before my eyes. I tried to get to her, stop the bleeding, stop her dying but I couldn't move, I couldn't go any further. This is just a picture show, slides of moments gone by. There is nothing you can do now.

I turned around and walked out the door, out of our small house in Clearwater, and into our front yard that was melting into a desert. On the horizon I could see Johnston's house and I ran for it.

Then I found myself standing in the kitchen. There were noises coming from underneath the stove, from the basement. I don't want to go down there again.

I went through a small door, through a narrow pantry, down a thin rotten flight of stairs, but this would be different, right? The stench from the old lady's closet assaulted me like a poisonous cloud and I started to gag. This was not the basement I had visited so many times before.

But the screaming was the same and I knew she was here. I started to run, I would find her this time and fix this, stop her pain and save her.

The white metal door, the knob was cold but it opened.

I saw my Mother. I can't do this. I'm sick with this. Someone was bent over her, on top of her and she was pleading from underneath him, was begging him and he wouldn't stop. I was starting to move towards him, not thinking anymore, just feeling this surge of hot hate, when my Mom's voice changed, the pitch was different and when I looked down to see her it wasn't, instead it was Gila.

Why the fuck would I dream this? I want to rip these pages out, burn them so it's like I never wrote them or thought them. Then this could never be true, right?

June 18, Friday 9:15 PM

I guess I should write on the progress of the mural first, get it over with and get to the interesting stuff.

I got in early, found my money and continued to work on the portrait of Johnston. I was at it for a couple of hours. I worked on some more sketches, went to lunch, went back to painting for a while longer.

It was about 5:00 when I decided to call it a day. I was cleaning off my brushes when I heard the front door open. I was in the hallway so I couldn't see who it was but a couple of seconds later a face peered around the corner, it was Razor's. He shot me that look and smiled, then slid back around and pounded up the stairs.

Reason said, don't even think about it, but I had to, so I did. I followed him up the stairs. He went into Johnston's office and shut the door. Crap. But I could still hear voices coming through so I hung back on the stairs and listened.

"Sit down," Johnston cleared his meaty throat, "We need to straighten some things out, there seems to be some confusion."

Silence for a couple of seconds then, "Simms found Slather in the warehouse. Would you happen to know anything about this?"

More silence.

"I know it was you. I want some answers. Doctor?"

Then I heard that laugh again. It was just like the time when he gutted Slather like a fish. Chills ran up my neck.

"You find this amusing?"

"Hysterical."

"He was a valuable asset to this family!"

"Fuck your family. He's lucky I let him live that long." The laughter was gone from Razor's words. Now he sounded cold and measured. I liked it better when he thought things were funny.

Then I heard a noise like a groaning squeak, like a drawer being opened.

"It's not there," then the Doc started to giggle again and all I could picture was Johnston searching for a gun gone missing.

"Unacceptable!" Johnston roared and it shook the door. "This will be enough!" Then a crash as the phone clattered to the floor.

"You don't get it, do you, Johnston? I know what you've been doing to her."

"She's been doing what's been asked of her.

You were there when she agreed."

"Liar,"

Silence. I could only imagine the look Johnston

was getting, I wondered if his head hurt.

"The next time you decide to slide a needle into

her vein, I *will* open up another member of your

shit box family. No threats, pig," Razor's voice a

thick whisper. " And it looks like you're running a

little thin on family these days." Then the door

flung open and a blur of black rushed past me, the

green of his eye clipping me for a split second,

then turned away with the fast steps of his feet

down the stairs.

I hauled my ass back downstairs, grabbed what

things I could and slid out the front door.

I know he was talking about Gila. He wants to get her out too, but why can't he? If he's having such a hard time then what makes me think that I can?

June 20, Sunday 2:00 AM

I'll just start at the beginning. That should be easier.

I started on the Splint part of the mural, which took most of the day. I decided to wrap it up around 4:00, hit the hay early, I felt pretty burned out. I was cleaning my brushes in the kitchen when Splint sneaked up behind me. He smelled terrible, drunk, I'm sure. What the hell does this guy do all day? He smelled even worse when he opened his mouth to ask me, "Up for some fun tonight, Chucky?"

Not with you, asshole.

"Come on, let's get you a drink," Splint smiled. God, I wished he wouldn't do that. I wondered if he was going to slip me one of those GHB's or something. We walked into the dinning room where he had a bottle of whiskey waiting and poured me a glass. I slugged it down, I had a bad feeling I was going to need it.

He was looking at me with this sneaky, sideward stare, "What's your poison?"

"What?"

"What gets your rocks off, ya know?" He poured himself another glass, "Boys? Girls? Little girls?" He laughed at that one. Private joke I guess.

Fuck this beat around the bush shit. I didn't quite know what he was hinting at, so I wanted to make it perfectly clear. "I'm straight."

He quit smiling and slowly turned his pink stained eyes towards me, "Well, I hope you're opened minded at least. Your gonna have to be for tonight, and there's no backing outta this one. The boss man wants you there."

Well, I have to say I felt incredibly uncomfortable but intrigued at the same time.

I went back to the hotel room and showered, dug out the only nice shirt I brought with me, and left around 7:30, making it back to the house fifteen minutes later.

I was nervous. I really didn't know what to expect. I could see people knocking on the door, going in. Couples, individuals, groups, some dressed up, some not.

I got to the door and slid by with a guy who had just been let in. I followed him into the mysterious green room. I took a seat at the small bar on the other side of the long space. I ordered whiskey on the rocks and noticed that the guy bartending was the skinny little guy Gila had thrown out of the room that night.

The place was getting filled up with people. There were men in suits, wealthy and cocky looking, then the ultra- mod, swinger types in silk shirts and leather pants. There were women everywhere. Lot's of them were beautiful. Blondes, redheads, every flavor, painted and done up. I think the majority of them were hookers.

I got up and walked around by myself, studying the various people, listening to their conversations, smelling their perfume and inhaling their smoke. I slowly made it to the little green stage. It was covered up tight with the velvet curtains.

"Hope you have that open mind, Chucky." I turned around to Splint's squinty, blood shot eyes.

He winked and spun around in the crowd to walk the other way. Weird fucker.

How did I get here? This whole situation seemed so unreal. I was beginning to forget why I came. I can't forget that. My mind was racing through all the people I had met so far, who had brought me to this place, all the things that have happened. Why did these things happen? I can't help but feel like I'm being led or pushed into these situations. Something stronger than me, something high up watching things coming together and making sure I'm there, right smack dab in the middle of it all. Deep thoughts, until something blonde caught my eye.

Platinum blonde to be exact, she blinded me for a second, gleaming in the greenish glow of the room. She had huge tits, perfectly round and packed tight in her crimson dress, and she had lips

to match, swollen and painted a glossy, rich candy

apple red.

Then from my right I heard the greasy, flab

filled laugh of Johnston. I spotted him sitting in a

green leather chair, dressed in the same white suit.

There was a skinny redhead sitting on his lap and

his fat mitt of a hand was shoved up her skirt, she

giggled, pretending to like it.

I spotted Splint at the bar, throwing back a shot

of something purple. He looked wrecked, skin

flushed in a healthy shade of yellow, he resembled

something from *The Evil Dead* as I watched him

start to pace back and forth, hands jammed in his

pockets.

I was thinking that this would make a really

interesting painting. Maybe I would put this in the

mural. Everything seemed magnified, the faces, the colors. Who were all these people and why were they here?

It seemed that a lot of the people were taking seats and I noticed most of the couches were filled to capacity. I could feel something in the room, tense expectation, like hearing thunder far off and faint but knowing it was coming closer and wondering how bad the storm would be. Something was about to happen.

I could see that a group of people that were standing in front of the doors were now moving to the side, letting someone through. A weird hush came over the crowd and some of the faces showed an intense hunger. Interesting. I moved closer to see.

I could see the crowd was letting something

lean, shiny and black into the room. She slithered

in like a gleaming oiled snake, every inch of her

tall, muscular body covered in leather, except for

her face. She reminded me of one of those women

in the B-grade Nazi flicks; incredible dark blue

eyes, flawless white skin, and of course the shock

of blonde hair, bound up tight in a long ponytail

running down a straight, strong back wrapped

perfectly in black.

She was holding something in her gloved hand. I

saw that it was a chain and I followed it until it

connected with a pair of bound hands of a young,

thin girl, probably about eighteen or nineteen. She

was totally naked and her skin was pale, almost

cloudy, her face gaunt and haunted, gagged with

something black that forced her jaw open at a strange angle. She kept her eyes down.

The two made their way to Johnston and I followed along with a bunch of other people all migrating to the tiny stage. I could see him watching her come closer, pushing the redhead off his lap and working himself out of the leather chair. I stopped and blended in with a group of people standing close by.

"Gretel! Gretel, welcome..." It was like he couldn't get there fast enough, as he waddled at top speed knocking people aside, slowing up to slip beside the Nazi. "Ah," his eyes going greedy, "the product. Good. It looks nice and broken."

I assumed that he meant she was 'broken' like a horse. That hit me in the chest, I wasn't sure what to think. Should I be here looking at them, witnessing this? Something in my psyche was quickly coming up with some kind of justification for staying and watching. *She let this happen, this is her choice.* I just couldn't believe it all the way.

Gretel raised one perfect eyebrow, "You've always had a taste for the defeated flesh." Her voice had a soothing musical tone to it. "I want this one back alive. She may not mind but she's no good to me dead."

What kind of fucking party was I at?

Johnston took his greedy eyes off the girl and focused on Gretel. "Of course." He looked back at the crowd, "Quite a draw tonight, should be a fine show."

She continued to stare at him. Finally he looked back to her. "Will there be anything else, Gretel?"

"Where is she?" Her words direct, her icy blues unblinking and sharp.

"She has duties to attend, agreements to keep." He had to look away.

"The Doctor as well?"

Now his face tensed, he took his gaze from the crowd, snapped them onto hers, "I wouldn't ask any more questions, it's really none of your concern. In fact, I'm sure you know where he is and that he has told you all about his indiscretions of late." He wiped his gleaming forehead, "Tell him to be careful, Gretel, very careful."

Gretel's lip curled up just a little, the tiniest smirk on her face, "I'm always careful. You're the one playing with snakes, Johnston. Don't underestimate them," her leathered fingers went to a faint scar on the right side of her face I hadn't noticed before, it started at the outer edge of her icy eye and traveled down to the sharp line of her jaw. "It will be the last mistake you'll make. Jimmy, prepare her, please." And with that she turned away, dismissing him with the gesture.

Suddenly a tall and meaty guy in white orderly uniform walked up behind her, taking the chain from her hand, yanked it once and the thin girl followed him through a door by the side of the stage.

Gretel continued to walk back through the crowd, towards the double doors. Her seemingly perfect movements were so well oiled and smooth that I had to follow her. I had no choice.

She started to slow down as she approached the green couch that the platinum blonde was sitting on. I went around to the back, leaning against the wall, trying to blend in with the surroundings.

"May I?" That musical sound again.

Platinum nodded and moved over slightly, and Gretel slithered in. I started to lean in closer when a couple of idiots pushed their way between me and the couch, talking about their 'tats' and it was drowning out the conversation between Platinum and the Nazi. I slid past them, back around the front and positioned myself near the arm of the sofa, no longer behind them but more to the side. Now I could hear everything as I stood there holding my drink, looking off into the crowd.

"So this is where I met Vinnie, he's the one that got me in the business," Platinum was blabbering, she wasn't even looking at Gretel while she talked.

Suddenly Gretel's hand went to the woman's thigh, grabbing it firm, "You like to talk," Her musical tone had turned cold and Platinum had stopped yapping. "You do porn, I understand. But why do you do it?" Gretel seemed as if she wasn't expecting an answer, she moved closer to the dumb-struck girl. "I believe most people do things that other people want them to do...you do that too."

"Excuse me?"

"You're young and so you have limited experience, in fact, I believe you don't know yourself that well at all." Gretel's tone became mocking, she was trying to get a rise out of this girl. Platinum was looking at her in this 'yeah, whatever' like way.

"You fuck because people tell you to, I want to know why *you* want to, if you do at all. Know yourself, if you have the courage."

The blonde couldn't believe what she was hearing, "Look, I know why I do films, cause I'm good. Real good. I'm a professional, I like what I do." Platinum argued. "What do you do? Sit around at parties and play with peoples heads all night?"

Gretel's eyes flashed and her smile grew wide, "Obviously you like your head played with or you wouldn't be sitting here with me would you now, little girl?" Gretel moved in even closer, "Deep down you are dying, I can see it in your eyes, smell it on your skin. You take too many pills with too many drinks. I know this because that's *my* talent, I find you and then I fix you. Make you better than you ever imagined." Gretel was staring into her eyes, and Platinum was stunned or mesmerized, her face had gone pale. "Do you want to be fixed? Truly know yourself?"

Platinum was speechless. I wasn't sure if she would get up and run away or sit there and listen to what this lunatic was saying.

"You'll be dead soon, I know. There's a part of you that wants that. You'll never be able to please Daddy and he's taken so much from you. That's why you search for redemption in every bed, find another Daddy to make you clean."

Platinum had turned away from Gretel. The girl looked sick and shocked.

"But I can show you how to silence his voice in your head. I can show you, if you are willing to be remade." Gretel put her arm behind Platinum, "What do you have to lose?"

Platinum turned back fast and stared at Gretel, trying to find the wolf hiding inside her skin. "Oh no, no. I don't know who you are but I don't think so. Get the fuck away from me…." And she tried to get up.

Gretel grabbed her arm and forced her back down to the sofa, "Daddy is a persuasive one, isn't he?"

Platinum barred her teeth and started to raise her hand towards Gretel's face, but that didn't work out too well, instead Gretel hit it away and grabbed onto her thick hair. "You think you're so dangerous, huh, little girl?" She wrenched her head back sharply. Now people were starting to notice, I guess it was all part of the show…

"You are soft, fearful. Listen. Are you listening?"

Platinum's eyes were wide, she didn't move.

"If you would be willing to learn, I could teach you. Did you know you are like candy? Soft and sweet, and they all love candy eat it up till it's gone. I myself don't like candy. I prefer meat. Can you be meat? Because meat is both alive and dead at the same time. This is what I require." Gretel's words had a slight slur to them and her eyes were halfway closed. She wasn't making sense to me but for some reason they did to Platinum, her eyes were closed too and her face lost that panicked look to it.

The noise level in the room was rising and I could barely make out what Gretel was saying to the woman. Something was about to happen and

109

everyone seemed excited, and it had nothing to do with what was happening on the couch to the side of me. I looked over towards the stage and saw Johnston sitting again in his green leather chair. He had been watching me and was smiling, amused I guess and he gestured me over to him. "You know, Charlie, you really should mind your own business." He said once I made it over to him, "Better find a seat, the show's about to begin."

I looked back over my shoulder to the couch but they both were gone. Did that really happen? It was getting easier and easier to say that these days. Then I caught a glimpse of shiny black moving through the crowd. I followed. I was moving up close behind them when I spotted Splint sitting in a green plastic chair next to the double doors. Gretel stopped in front of him and he glanced up, a look of pure anguish appeared on his pasty face.

"Well, well…hello, Splint," Gretel purred, "What's wrong? Lizard got your tongue?" Then she laughed, no, *cackled* would be a better description, she sounded evil. Splint looked up, a vile gaze aimed at her but she was already gone, out the doors with Platinum at her side. He looked more miserable than I had ever seen him, as he pried himself from the chair and headed for the bar.

Just then the lights faded and I noticed that most of the people had found seats. I decided to stick close to the doors, just in case.

I could see the little stage in the corner was glowing softly, lit from within, casting weird emerald shadows on the people sitting in front. The curtains slowly opened.

There on the stage, standing naked and alone was the thin girl that had come in on the chain with Gretel. Her head was tilted down, staring at her feet, her hands tied together with tight black straps.

From the back of the stage came Jimmy, naked as the day he was born too, but stylin' some black rubber gloves and a lone ranger mask. I noticed he was holding his floppy dick in one hand, encouraging its attention.

I looked down at the sitting participants and saw that a silver bowl was being passed between them, full of little bits of paper. Then the bowl was handed to Jimmy, he took it with the hand that wasn't busy. He took it to a small table that was sitting on the far end of the stage, put it down and took one of the bits of paper from it.

I looked back over at the thin girl, still staring at her feet. Her tits were small, perky with tiny pink nipples. Should I be doing this? I kept thinking this in my head. Did I have any right to be there, looking at this girl's tits? My eyes panned down, she was really thin, I could see her ribs outlined under her pale skin, she reminded me of a stray dog. I could see that she was shaved bald, but not recently, I noticed the stubble starting to poke through between her thighs.

Was this turning me on? Usually someone like this wouldn't, I'm not into strung out, skinny girls. Give me an Eric Stanton chick, something tall and curvy with big tits, but skinny like this made me feel sorry for her. I guess the one thing that was somewhat of a turn-on was the suspense of what would come up next.

I caught Jimmy moving closer towards the girl then circling her. His dick was standing up on its own and he dragged it on her body as he circled, along her stomach, hip, back.

She still wasn't moving.

Then he started to whisper into her face, ear, back of head. I wanted to know what those words were, I tried to read his lips but they moved too fast.

I caught a movement in her face, her eyes closed and the corner of her lip curved into an expression of relief.

What the fuck was he saying?

Jimmy raised his gloved hand to the girl's face, one going to her throat, locking itself underneath her chin. He squeezed and her mouth popped open, gasping for breath. His other hand grabbed at her stringy dishwater hair and twisted it up tight, wrenching her reddened face back with a jerk, finally releasing her throat while forcing her to her knees.

Her bound hands went to her neck as she gagged for air but Jimmy remedied that by cranking her head farther back, her neck arching painfully as he slipped himself into her gapping mouth.

"Don't you bite," his voice as thick and heavy as the arm that pushed her face deeper onto his cock. Using her hair to move her up and down, back and forth, faster and faster until his groaning filled the room. I could hear choking deep from her throat, and her cheeks gleamed with tears.

Cum and spit flew from her mouth as Jimmy pulled himself out, untangled his glove from her hair and pushed her head towards the floor. She lay there on her side coughing.

He walked back to the table and took another piece of paper from the bowl, opened it, nodded, threw it to the floor. He bent down and searched for something underneath the table. He pulled out something long and black. Shinny smooth jarred my memory, red and smeared above Splint's bed and he held it in his hands, fondling it. The rubber of his gloves was making creepy squeaky noises against it and it gave me the chills.

He walked over to the balled up girl, reached down, and grabbed her arm, yanked her to her knees.

"On your feet."

Jimmy watched her rise from the floor, slowly stroking the club. He circled her again, gently touching her with it, rolling it down her back, across her stomach, running it between her tits. He then brought it to her face, and her lips parted, tongue sliding out to taste it, leaving the tip of the club coated shiny with spit. Jimmy traced it back over her stomach, down to the stubble, and then through her skinny thighs. Moving it faster and faster, in and out, while he watched her face intently.

Maybe this wouldn't be as bad as I thought it would be.

She let out a small moan.

Jimmy ripped the club out from between her legs and slammed it into her stomach. She went to her knees, doubling over when Jimmy decided to bring the club down hard on her spine and I heard a muffled crack. She fell on her face.

Christ on a mountain. I had to look away but I heard another hit, another crack. I couldn't watch him do this, couldn't take part in this. I turned to the doors behind me but there were people blocking the way, people watching this, people liking this.

Call it compulsion or extreme optimism but I looked back to the stage. He was back at the bowl, picking out another piece of suggested pain and suffering, and tossing it to the floor. The thin girl was on her stomach not moving but there was a growing puddle of blood from underneath her face. I couldn't tell if she was still breathing.

Did she know that this would be happening to her? What was happening?

I had to get the fuck out of there. I pushed my way through the crowd of mesmerized people all the way to the closed French doors. I looked back one last time.

Never should have done that.

Jimmy stood over thin girl who was now flipped onto her back. He straddled her, while jacking off with a knife in his hand screaming into her face that he was "Gonna make new holes...".

I turned the handle and stumbled out the doors into the foyer and out the front into the moist, cool night. I kept going, into the car, down the road, into my hotel room.

Was this a test? I think so. They wanted to see how much I could take, if I was into this. If I was like them. Am I? Why did I stay so long? Watching him kill her, why did I look back?

I feel infected. Maybe I did like it. It looked like a game, like no one would get hurt, right? I should have helped her, call the cops, something. Why didn't I?

Then something black and rotten bubbles up from some forgotten, hidden fissure in my mind and it starts to laugh. It looks at me with unblinking, bottomless eyes, burning me through with its darkened glare and it gurgles, "Because you are just like them."

Sometimes I scare myself.

6:15 AM

What the fuck is going on? Something really wrong, I know, I'm losing it, like everything coming apart. I never should have stayed, or looked, or anything. I'm being punished for it. I know it. Where the fuck was Reason when I needed it?

I just woke up from a nightmare, what the fuck else is there these days?

I'm riding in the passenger side of a car, staring out the window and watching the lights floating in the surrounding dark. I look over at the driver and see Slather at the wheel. I feel strange, disconnected.

"What if he comes back, walks in on us?" Slather glancing over at me with nervous, feral eyes. I have a sudden urge to hit him, like bashing his head into the steering wheel, just for being a fucking pussy.

"Fuck that, who cares? Let him watch," I tell him, and then I laugh high pitched and fast. This isn't my mouth, not my sounds. This isn't me.

"Yeah, I guess you're right, it's only Razor." His hands squeezing the wheel tight, sweat cascading down his pocked marked cheek. What a fucking loser.

The car stops in front of Gristoff's hotel. We get out and my hand goes to the inside of my coat pocket and I feel it there, all cold, smooth and heavy, I grip it and my mouth goes dry and my chest begins to pound. "This will be good, " I murmur to myself. Who am I?

Slather is standing next to a door, his hand on the knob and I feel my throat closing up and it's hard to swallow and I'm wondering how long it's gonna take that fucking retard to open it.

We barge into the room like fucking superheroes, the light bright and it stings a little. But I still could see and what I see is her standing there in a white T-shirt and nothing else.

"Here lizard, lizard, lizard,"

She stands staring at me, in total shock, like a deer in headlights. I rush forward, grab her by the arm, and it makes me really mad that she was standing there like that, like some kind of fucking idiot. "Hey, Slather, look what we got here, Razor's pet lizard!"

Slather is sitting on the bed, opening his little fun bag full of smack.

"One sec, Splint."

Splint? Oh God.

I'm peering into her face, and she's breathing hard and her dark eyes are all scared, so sad. Oh fucking well. This is it, bitch. Fucking Superman is here and has come to save your sad fucking day. Sad, sad, sad. God, I want to hurt her. I can't wait to hear her scream. She starts to pull away from me, like she doesn't want to be so close or something. Nope, don't think so and I grip her tighter and bring her closer to me. Finally, she starts to scream so I let her a little, like I said I like the sound of it, of all that fear and sad and then I can't wait any longer and hit her right in that pretty little mouth of hers. Yeah, that was good. Now there's blood dripping from her swollen lip and things are really coming together.

My dick hurts because it's so tight in my pants now and I needed to start this rolling. I rip at her shirt, and I can see her tits swinging around so I grab at them and squeeze as hard as I can and she screams louder than before. I hit her again. She needs this, she needs me to show her what a stupid little cunt she is and that I'm in control now. I'm gonna give it to her, give her what she needs. I'm sweating and I feel lightheaded, I need to slow this down a little, make it last.

I feel her push at me, like she thinks she's gonna get away. Right. I like it when they fight a little, struggle, it gets me hotter. I take her and throw her to the ground and now she's underneath me all squirming and thrashing around. You can't get away, I'm too strong. You're mine now, and you won't forget it.

"Looks like you got a wild one." Slather's voice slurred and stupid. He comes around and gets hold of her arms, stretching them above her head.

I have all my weight on her now and she's really starting to panic. She tries turning her head away from me but I grab her face and make her look at me. She screams. Now she knows me, she would know me forever. I have top spot in her mind, I can jump out of the darkest corners of her dreams, even the good ones, or whenever she would feel the slightest tinge of happiness I will be there, and she will think of our special time together. I will ruin her.

If I decide not to kill her...

I'm in control now. I'm unzipping my jeans and she's looking away again so I turn her face to make her watch what I'm taking out and her eyes are all far away, like she doesn't care. I'll make

her care. So I ram it in and it's so tight and I feel it

giving away, things ripping and now she's

screaming again and it's all muffled and sexy

through the shirt in her mouth. I want to blow my

load right now but I have control. I fall on top of

her, my face in her dark hair so warm and soft. I

find her ear and bite it, taste the blood. She

squirms as hard as she can, but she can't get away.

This is so good, but all good things must pass and

I can feel it building again, coming closer.

Shooting it into her, I can feel it flood her, filling

her full. Poisoning every wrinkle, spoiling every

secret space that she tried to keep from me.

Done.

I pull out quick and stand up. "She's all yours." I

don't want to look at the mess on the floor. She's

starting to make me sick and I really want to get the fuck out of here.

I don't even know or care what the hell Slather is doing, what he even could do. I keep looking at my watch, not midnight yet but close. Almost time to bring her back to the house. I look back at her. She lay there on the tacky red carpet, not moving. I got an idea.

"Hey, you still got that shitty horse?"

Slather looks at me and nods and goes for the fun bag. I'm not done with this whore yet, I'm gonna give her the time of her life before I'm through.

Slather stands there with a needle in his hand, "But what about Hildy? Won't she be pissed if we bring her in all fucked up?"

What a pussy. "Look, I don't want her

screaming and pitching a fit when we're bringing

her back. Do you?"

"No. Guess not." He sits on the floor next to her.

I reach into my pocket again, and feel the

smooth cold of the metal, slipping it out so

carefully. The feel of the knife giving me another

hard on. Superman baby.

I lower myself to the floor. I put my hand on her

thigh and she wakes up, scrambling like a crab,

away from me, but I still have hold of her leg and

drag her back, Slather drops the needle to grab a

hold of her too. I go for her arm but she's stronger

than I give her credit for. I can't keep her still. I

find myself between her legs again and I feel the

need coming back strong. My hand is sliding up

her thigh, into blood and cum, through the tightness and the swelling.

Slather has hold of her arms again, but she's really thrashing around. I go to hold down her other leg and I feel pressure on the knife, then a flood of warmth and a loud scream from the slut. I look down and see blood everywhere cause the blade had cut the inside of her thigh.

"Goddamn it, Splint! Shoot her up!"

I'm having a hard time holding her down. The gash in her leg is deep, the three inch blade has gone half way through her leg. There's blood everywhere.

Fuck. What to do? At least I don't have to worry about the blood, this was Gristoff's place, he would deal with it. Then I start to feel her relax a little, she's letting up because of all the bleeding. The carpet gleams with it.

"Her veins will be shit after this, man." The fuck was right. She had lost too much blood, it will be impossible to hit anything in her arm. I find the needle that he had dropped and go for her sliced thigh. I slide the needle into the gash as far as it will go and push the plunger. I take the shirt from her mouth and wrap it around her leg, then take the sheet from the bed and throw it over her.

"Get her in the car."

That's when I woke up.

I have this weird feeling, like someone sitting beside my bed while I'm sleeping, whispering things, turning into nightmares when the words hit my brain.

It was her. I don't want to hurt her, never did. I want to get her out of that house, now more than ever.

Splint. I can't even think about him without wanting to puke. All of this... his thoughts, his laugh and words. Not mine. Right?

A part of me has given up and surrendered to the notion that this might be something else, that all these dreams are more than dreams, they're pieces of a puzzle, a story. Something other than the bleak option that I might be as fucked up and twisted as the green room people, infected with a sickness that craves the pleas and tears of dying girls.

But I keep going back to the feel of Gila underneath me, and I don't want to admit that it felt good, that somehow now I know her well, that

I have a piece of her here with me, and it gives me some sense of control. It's not right, I know. These thoughts are unhealthy and polluted. I need to purge them, forget them then maybe I can feel clean again. Maybe.

June 21, Monday 5:30 PM

I'm surprised I made it to work today, after my
nervous breakdown last night, this morning, or
whenever it was. I got to the house around 11:00. I
really had no intention of painting anything, I just
walked around, replaying all the shit that's been
running rampant in my head from that nightmare.

Except for Splint, no one was around, if he even
counts for anything. I couldn't even look at him. I
decided that I had to get out of the house. Splint
wasn't good for the psyche and the heat was
getting hotter. I thought the gardens would be a
good place to go.

There was a path made out of flagstone and it
seemed to spiral inward, big loops, into the green
confusion of the vegetation. The plants calmed me

a little, took my mind off things. I walked for awhile, couldn't tell how long, just walked trying not to think too much. All of a sudden I found myself standing at the edge of a small clearing. I was a little disorientated; I had no idea that a large space like this could exist within the middle of the spiral. It was definitely a strange place, everything there was very still, no wind, no birds, just calm.

I stood there listening and I could feel myself getting tired, I really wanted just to sit down and I noticed a lone tree in the center of the clearing. Low and small, its branches hung thick and almost touched the ground in some spots. I walked over to it and sat down inside its shadow of shade.

Then, well, I don't remember anything else until she started to shake me.

"Wake up!"

My head was throbbing and I tried to open my eyes that were all goopy and stuck together. All I could see was a bright smear of blue.

"Hey wake up!"

I tried to say that I was, but there was no spit to lubricate the words, and they came out in some kind of garbled mess. Then I heard her laugh.

I rubbed my eye and looked again. It was the old woman I had seen the other day. The one Splint didn't see. She was bending down in front of me, her wrinkled face kind, her bright blue eyes flashed in the afternoon light. I was happy to see her.

"How did you manage to fall asleep out here in this heat?" Her words were tinged voodoo smooth, Hatian maybe? "Here, drink this," and she handed me a glass full of something wet and wonderful, and gulped it down without thinking about what it actually might be. I think it was water but it was sweeter.

I handed her back the glass and extended my hand, "Thank you. I'm Charlie."

"Hailey," and she took my hand and squeezed. Her smile reminded me of my Grandmother's, the way she would stare at me across the table at dinnertime, and then she would ask me how my day was, because I remember that's when my days were getting better. I missed her a lot right then, and I wondered what she would be doing. I really should call her but my minutes had all but run dry many moons ago. I reached into my shirt pocket for my smokes and saw Hailey looking at me.

"Would you like one?" I offered.

"Yes. Please. Very good."

I lit one, handed it to her, and she took a deep drag. We just sat there for a couple of minutes, not talking, only smoking, but it wasn't weird or uncomfortable. It was kinda nice.

"Are these your gardens?"

Her face lit up as she looked around. "In ways." Her eyes were playful, like she really didn't plan on giving me the answer to that question. "I have been caring for these gardens for many years now. You can say I've always been here. What brings you here, Charlie?"

"Well the house was getting a little hot, so I decided to take a walk."

She laughed and shook her head, "No, why are you here, in this place?"

"Oh, um… I'm here to paint a mural for Mr. Johnston."

"Is that all?"

"What do you mean?" I was confused. I

shouldn't take naps.

She turned to face me fully, she looked like she

was about to explain something really complicated

to a little kid. "How did you come to be in this

place?" What brought you here?"

My mind raced through all the reasons and

images and intentions. She really wanted to know

this? Should I tell a total stranger the real reasons

why I'm here? She didn't feel that strange so,

what the fuck. She smiled and I laughed, took a

deep breath. "Tell me," she urged.

I hadn't told this story in years. I'd hoped I'd

never have to tell it again. I was always afraid that

if I did, it would be like picking at an old scab, and

instead of healthy pink underneath, it would be all

black and bloody. Then I would have to face facts, it would not get better, it would never heal.

I was twelve years old and I lived in the small town of Clearwater, Louisiana. I was an only child.

Times weren't so great back then. My dad wasn't working, and he and my mom fought all the time. They decided to send me away to my grandmother's for the summer, up in Chicago. They told me that they needed time to find my dad a job and get some things straightened out. That scared me. They had never fought like that and there had never been times like those before and for the first time in my life things were uncertain and I was being sent away. But they said not to worry and that they loved me and I would see them soon.

The summer marched by and I did have a good time with Gram. But seven days before I was to go back home, the carp of death found me on the banks of my sanctuary, whispering with stinking breath that good things would not come of this, then four days after that Gram opened the door to two cops. They explained to her that my mom, her daughter, had committed suicide. I remember standing there in the hallway focusing on the dark blue of their hats, listening to the alien sounds of grief and disbelief of my grandmother, and coming to my own conclusion that they had the wrong address.

They said that the police in Louisiana found my mom in our house, her wrists cut and a note in her hand, a letter from my father saying that the love was gone and another woman was in his life.

I know I ran full force at the cops, trying to shove them out the door. They needed to find the right house, tell the right people. They needed to leave us alone. I don't remember anything else, until her funeral.

I couldn't believe that my dad would do that. That he could just leave us like that. But Gram did and she hated him bitterly and there was nothing I could do about it. I know she wanted me to hate him too, but I couldn't.

My dad never made it to her funeral on that hot, horrid day in September. I waited and waited but in my gut I knew he wouldn't come and I knew then that they were wrong about him. He didn't run off, he wasn't with another woman, and if he could, he would have come to her funeral and took me home. There was more to this, there had to be.

That's when I started to worry a lot, when the anxiety began. Over the next few years came the shrinks and the long, long talks and when that didn't quite work, they introduced me to the tranquilizers and the sedatives, padding my thoughts and killing my short-term memory.

Gram was always there for me though, and we went through it together. When I think about it, I don't know how we made it through. She's all I've got left.

But it never set right with me. I always wondered about my dad, where he was and why my mom was dead. I tried my best to ignore it, pop another pill, but it still stayed. By the end of high school, I had weaned myself off the drugs, well, cut back anyway. I decided on art school, so

I went, going downtown everyday, but I got bored with it by the end of the year.

Then three months ago the dreams started, images of my mom screaming in cold, spider-filled basements, and the after taste of mildew and old rotten memories. Something told me to go back, to see what I could find, that there were things I should see. I still don't know what those things would be.

"So, that's my story."

Hailey nodded, her eyes filled with concern, then she reached over and patted my hand, "You have another cigarette?" She smiled sweetly.

I lit another one for her. She took a few drags and looked at me, "So you came here?"

"Yeah, I think I took a wrong turn somewhere."

"No, you are here for a *reason*. There's always a *reason*." She winked a watery blue eye at me and smiled. "What would be the reason then, Charlie? What brought you here to the house of Johnston?" And her smile faded, like a cloud passing over the bright of day.

I've been wondering that myself these days. "I stopped at a hotel in town and was offered a job to paint a warehouse but that didn't last long." I tried to suppress the slideshow of blood and gore projected in my head. "Then Johnston's doctor set me up with a job position here, painting the mural."

"Razor," she whispered it and when I snapped my head around to look at her, she was staring up into the sky.

"You know him?"

She redirected her gaze down at her feet that were bare and entwined with the grass, "Yes I do. Do you?" Tricky again, that smile creeping across the wrinkles.

"Well, kind of, I mean I've seen him around, he's got these really weird eyes. You've seen them, right?"

"Some say he can see through the lie, see into the hiding truth," her voice was different now and she seemed so far away. "Green eyes born of a second sight, a green from down below."

"What?" She lost me.

"Or he may just be a doctor, nothing else."

I knew something was up with him, I knew because I felt it, that green stare sliding into my skull when he spoke to me, that voice that came from nowhere. I decided to approach her from another angle.

"I also saw a woman upstairs. Can you believe this, she was actually chained to a bed!"

"Gila," her voice was so clear, it rang like a bell, say it again, say it a million times. "I know how much you think about her, how much your need has grown."

Wow, how did she know this? "That obvious?" I tried to shake it off, play it cool. My head was spinning, what was happening?

"She's been calling to you," Hailey whispered into my burning ear and I froze.

"What did you say?" I could barely talk.

She put an arm around my shoulder and gave me a squeeze, "You need to know more, I know. Tonight, when the sun starts to fade, come back to me, right here in this spot. I will tell you all you need to know." She stood up, extended her hand, and pulled me up. "And bring some rum."

Pretty bizarre, huh? The logical side of my brain is asking me some pretty significant questions about all this; What if this is some kind of joke? What if I get there and everyone I've met so far on this creepy little get away is there waiting in that field, and they either are there to kill me or laugh their asses off at me for believing all this *mumbo-jumbo*. Well, yeah I tend to agree with these possibilities but then there's that other voice, and it reminds me of all the dreams and all the weird stuff that has happened to bring me here, to this spot and how I would be an idiot not to follow through.

June 22, Tuesday 2:00 PM

I don't know where to begin. I'm still trying to figure out all of this but I can't. I'm not even sure where I'm at exactly.

I'm getting off the path. I need to focus on the story in my head. All the things that saw me, or that I saw…

I left the hotel last night, right before dark. I had the bottle of rum Hailey had asked for and I brought some cans of Coke along for good measure. I was excited, anxious, and happy all at the same time. I was going to learn what I needed to know, all about her, about Gila.

Gila.

I reached the field as the sun went down. The clearing wasn't quiet anymore. Things buzzed and

149

squealed, rustled and growled in the dark of the trees. Things were waking up, restless wild things, and it was making me jumpy. I looked around, no one there. Where was she?

I walked across the field, to a thick curve of vegetation that stopped my progress. I peered into the tress and saw something solid with straight lines inside. I pushed myself through and came to a shack, barely standing, faded and pieced together. Then I heard a squeak of a rusty hinge, then a pale flood of yellow light.

"You made it," Hailey stood there. A small lantern in one hand, "did you bring the rum?"

"Hey, yeah right here. It really got dark fast, huh?"

I followed her into the purple gloom. We came back to the edge of the clearing. She wasn't saying anything; in fact, she kept walking farther and farther out into the open space. I tried to keep up with her, see where I was going, until she finally stopped at the small tree that I had taken a nap under earlier that day.

"Charlie," she turned to face me and she looked a little different, but I couldn't put my finger on it. "What is it that you have come here for?" The whites of her eyes shined in the blackness.

"You told me you were going to tell me all I need to know."

She brought her hands to my face, "Yes, but what do *you* need to know? You need to tell me this."

What did I want? I wanted her to tell me that this wasn't some waking nightmare, that I wasn't crazy. I wanted to know everything, why I was here, who she was.

"Tell me about her," I felt the words push out hot and greedy. "Give me Gila."

I saw the shadow of her grin spread over her face like a ghost. "Yes, yes, but with every want comes a price. Can you name my price?" Her voice lower, throaty. Price?

"What do you want?"

She took her hands from my cheeks and stepped back. "Anything I ask." The humor was gone, the apparition fading from her face. I shivered.

"Do you believe in the powers of the flesh? Of the unseen world?"

She was staring at me waiting for an answer. "Yes." I barely murmured it. Why was she asking me this?

"Take my hand, and follow my step." So I did, and we walked back across the field, through the thick of the leaves, to the little shack. She pushed open the door.

The yellow of the lantern bounced off a portion of the shack inside and everything it touched appeared harsh, angry, and angular. She turned around.

Okay, how to put this…she was different. My first reaction was that someone else was in the shack with us, and now that person was standing in front of me. This wasn't Hailey. Daughter maybe. Her hair was more black than silver, and it spilled out from underneath the blue bandana. Her eyes were more defined. Her skin was less wrinkled.

"Give me the rum."

I held it out with a shaky hand and she took it and winked. I watched her walk over to a bench in the middle of the room and she carefully placed it with some other bottles. She was mumbling something softly and she went down on her knees. As I started to walk towards her I could see all sorts of covered jars, flowers, and shadowy figures of owl-like creatures with huge eyes.

"Hailey?"

Her head flung around to meet my voice, "One final question, Charlie." Slowly standing to peer into my eyes. "Do you have a vulnerable soul? Because that is what I need."

"Vulnerable?" It came out weak and thin. What the hell was I getting into? She waited for an answer so I nodded yes.

She took my hand again and led me to a pole
that stood a little ways back from the bench. It was
painted in bright colors that ran up the length of it,
like a barbers pole.

"Take off your shoes."

I reached down and fumbled with the laces and
pulled them off, wondering what she was going to
have me do next. I looked up to see that she had
faded into the darkness. Then a small movement
of light, then another, and another as she lit
candles and a soft, gradual brightness filled the
rest of the room, shadows licked at the walls.

But between the shadows were the colors, weird
shapes and symbols, painted on the uneven planks
of the walls. I was trying to comprehend some of
those patterns when she pushed me against the
pole. I looked into her face and instantly denied

what I saw, closed my eyes, and waited for the hallucination to fade. Reason whimpered that it was just the light from the candles, playing tricks with her face. I opened my eyes.

She stood smiling at me, taking the bandana away from her hair and long, thin, black braids fell down to her shoulders, no traces of silver at all. She shook her head and looked down.

"I may look another age to the outside world, but here I am who I am." Her skin was smooth like that of a thirty-year old woman's. How could this be?

"Don't ask too many questions. You may be disappointed."

There were too many of those questions and I'm sure no good answers. I noticed she had a glass in her hand, full of something milky white and shimmering.

"Drink this."

I was afraid she was going to say that. I took it from her hand. What was it? Did I want to know? Well maybe just a taste. I brought it to my lips and a little of it slid into my mouth. It was thick and sweet and instantly my mouth watered for it, my lips closed around the cool of the glass as I gulped it down. I couldn't get enough of it and it coated my tongue thick with a craving that I couldn't satisfy, I couldn't drink it fast enough. I started to feel instant warmth in my stomach and that's when she pulled the glass from my lips.

I felt lightheaded and I started to sweat. I looked around for something to grab hold of and that's when I noticed the lines in the dirt, white and chalky, swirled and circled, like snakes twisting around my feet.

"Are ya still willing to know?" She breathed cool and soft into my face.

"Yes." I heard myself say from far away.

Then she took my hand and it felt different, like electric going through my arm, making my hairs stand on end. She led me to the back of the shack, to another door. She opened it and I could smell dirt, rich and damp, then the scent of flowers, familiar, I knew this, but couldn't think on it. She led me out into the thick night air and I could feel the cold wet of grass underneath my feet, the smooth brush of leaves against my arms.

We stopped at another door, smaller and made of rusty metal. She pushed it open. Instantly there was light and heat and it was coming from hundreds of flickering candles. I looked up and around and that's when I saw them. The colors.

Incredible. I had never seen colors like this, rich, pulsating, thick, alive. The indigo and violets felt like plush velvet, shining with cool texture, multifaceted and translucent. They formed more designs, swirling and complex, and they seemed to pull at my lungs, making breathing difficult.

She turned me around, disconnecting me from the walls. "Remember to breath," she said, but I couldn't, not after what I saw in front of me. She stood there, the youngest yet, early twenties maybe. Skin perfect like dark cream. She made me thirsty. I stood there, unbelieving. Then she stepped away from me and let her dress fall to the dirt.

"Come to me, Charlie. Come love this loa."

Loa? Didn't matter. Such a soft voice coming from such a pretty mouth. I took her in, my eyes moved over curves, over heavy tits, smooth stomach, in between full thighs. Fuck, I wanted her bad. I couldn't think, didn't think. Only wanted to touch her, get close and lose myself in her.

She moved to a table, popped herself on top and spread her legs. I was ripping at my clothes, tripping over my shorts. Finally I reached her and rushed to her lips, my mouth closing over hers, soft, sweet. I slid myself into her wetness and pushed hard. I felt her press into me, pulling me into her. It was too much, sensory overload and I almost lost it. My blood was on fire and my balls were burning and I was there and I needed to pull out, real quick before…wait, did I? I felt her hand on my ass, keeping me inside, and I thrust deeper.

"Give it to me," she groaned in my ear. So I did.

I remember laying there in the dirt with Haley in my arms and thinking what the hell had just happened, who this was. But here she was, young, soft and firm in my hands. I don't know how, I don't think I want to know yet. I knew I was losing my mind, I accepted it. I surrendered.

"Why don't you sleep a little bit?" Her soft murmur, head nuzzling into my chest. She was warm and I was pretty tired, so I did.

The first dream I had started with that horrible feeling of falling, faster and faster, through clouds and rushing air. The blur of brown quickly turned to rock below, but I never hit the ground. Instead I was standing in a desert, right before sunset and it was hot. Torrid heat shimmered off the rocks and sand, the light growing softer, purple.

Then I saw them, Razor and Gila, sitting in the sand, sweating, shivering. She was so much more real, I could see the drops of sweat roll down her skin, hear the grunts under her breath. She was holding Razor, burned pink and unconscious.

I looked behind me, way, way back in the purple stained hills, where a huge building was standing there white and gleaming and I felt a kick of fear in my gut. I turned back to Razor and Gila but they were gone.

I blinked the sweat from my eyes and opened them to a hospital room, dirty green and ugly light. She was there, huddled in a wrinkled bed, motionless. My stomach tensed when I comprehended her too pale face, when I looked into those vacant eyes and didn't see her there. Silent and shut down, she had been broken and no one was fixing her, no one could. How did I know this?

I couldn't watch this any longer so I walked through the door, right into another room, soft white with dim light, and he was there. Razor lay in a bed, lines and bottles dripping into his red and peeling arms.

Why was I here?

I opened my eyes for real, I think, to the soft light of candles and Hailey giving me head. This was nuts, but why question it?

Her mouth was soft and hot and she was doing these things with her tongue. I was about there,

163

when she pulled back and said, "I think you are ready," breathy and sweet. She climbed up and slid herself over me. Control, Hactor. Her fingers moved up across my chest to my neck then slithered up to my hair, through it and in it, entwined and twisted, pulling my head back until I was looking up at the ceiling.

"Do you wish I was her?" That breathy sweet again but with an edge. The image of Gila's bloody swollen lips polluted my thoughts. "You have bad things in you, Charlie. You think on bad things." Her fist tightened and my scalp burned. She raised herself up, so close to out and slid back down and squeezed. Control. I felt hard nipples on my chest as she clamped her mouth down on mine. I pushed my tongue through, into thick warmth, and she tasted as sweet as she sounded.

Then she disconnected and glared into my eyes.

"You have been in bad places, seen bad things."

That made me mad for some reason, and I reached up to grab hold of her, flipping her over. I took her arms and pinned them above her head, looked down at her and smiled, "I could show you, all the bad things." And pounded her hard while pictures of dark, fearful eyes and long open thighs flooded my head. Hailey moaned and wrapped her legs around my back. The images got clearer right before I came, they always do. I could smell the blood on the carpet, the shampoo in her hair, her panicked face drowning in tears. Then the free fall into oblivion, paired with the intense pull from her as she took it all from me again, draining me dry.

"What did you dream?"

The words vibrated through her chest and into my left ear that rested on her right tit. I opened my eyes.

"It was a dream that I had before. Gila and Razor in the desert, sweating and shaking."

She shifted under me, "That was the beginning of it all, in the desert."

"The beginning?"

She wrapped her arms around me and I felt so warm, so safe. "Close your eyes and let the pictures come. Listen to my words."

And with that I relaxed and let her voice rumble its rhythm, leading me into soft dark and liquid depth. I let go.

"How did you find me?"

She sat on a small narrow bed, her too dark eyes focused on Razor. Gila looked sick, still broken.

Razor fumbled with a bottle of pills, then looked up. "I knew where to look," and smiled. "I've been doing some research and I think I know how to make you well again."

She frowned, shaking her head, "If you want to help me Raze, do one thing. Make it stop. Stop the dreams."

I opened my eyes to her words and the shadows of the shack. I tried to get up, but she held me tighter, keeping me down. "Shhh. Now we come to a vital part. Close your eyes and do not be afraid. I have you."

I closed my eyes. I had no choice.

167

The pills weren't working. The dreams poked through her troubled sleep. He knew this. He could hear the fear, the resistance in her voice as she tossed and turned.

"I had a bad one, Raze." She whispered. "We were in a house, it was white and deathly. There was blood in the kitchen, the family there killed their cook and left him dying on the floor." She wept in his arms.

"I can try a stronger sedative, we'll see if that works." His face sagged with the worry of it. He didn't believe his own words.

"There's more." She looked up into his eyes, his dark brown eyes. Dark brown eyes. Dark brown eyes....

"His eyes, his eyes Hailey!" I struggled out of her embrace. Hallucinations, illusions, all lies and tricks! The color? Where was his green? What the hell was all this about? Wait…this was just a dream, right?

I got up and instantly fell back down, the room spun and my head hurt. I was confused and discombobulated. Hailey was next to me, pulling me down to her stomach, wrapping those arms around me one more time and I could feel her warmth again but without the safety.

"His eyes came later, much later. Stay calm and try not to disconnect from me."

"I don't understand, what am I seeing?" My voice sounded delayed and slow.

She started to stroke my hair, "Images of a story. Her tale of a gift turned into a burden, and she wanted it aborted."

"But why?" My eyes were getting heavier.

"Dreaming deaths and paying no heed to their warnings. The results left her torn and weeping."

I felt bad for her. I hoped Razor could do something. I hoped this story had a happy ending. Reason told me to stop being so naïve.

"So, where have you been spending all your extra time, Doctor?" Johnston smirked at him as he rolled up his sleeve, exposing the swollen, fish belly flesh of his arm.

Razor was drawing something into a small syringe, tapping it with a finger and approached Johnston. "Nowhere special," said quietly. Razor wrapped a thin rubber tube around Johnston's arm while searching for a vein, guessed, then stuck the needle in. Johnston's face slackened, features melted as he closed his eyes.

"I know where you've been," slurred words that made Razor jump, " and who you've been with. Be sure to tell me next time."

Razor said nothing as he put the bottle and needle into his shiny black bag.

"We're having a feast tomorrow night, breaking in a new cook. I want you to bring her." Johnston's words final and hard.

He would go back and explain to her what was expected of them, why they had to go.

"How did you come to be his doctor, Raze? What happened?"

He paced the floor of the small room, wringing

his hands, looking down at his feet. Gila got up

and grabbed his arms, but he wouldn't look at her.

"It got too hard. I lost it as a surgeon, I'm no

good, my nerves...well, you know my nerves. Now

I sew them up, all his thug family. I fix them and

give them drugs, they give me money. It's all I can

do."

He dropped down to his knees and gripped her

legs, face squeezed in between her calves,

"Forgive me, Gila."

Warm liquid was running down my throat, and

that incredible craving swelled inside my mouth

again.

"Forgive me, Gila," I heard myself say in

between the swallows. I wasn't in the room yet. I

was still watching Razor beg for mercy. It was weird. Two places at once.

He wept at her feet, shaking with the sobs. Humiliated, ashamed....

Bright colors bled through the scene as I started to wake up. I was hot, really hot, and she was rubbing my shoulders, then my back, chest, stomach. I felt greasy and I noticed that she had oil all over me, kneading it in, slick and shiny.

"Time to wake up." I felt her tight grip slip around my balls.

"I'm up!" My heart was pounding, blood pumping, surging at full speed through every vein, each limb, including what she held in her lubed up hand. Faster, tighter, then faster again, almost there, wait…control. Then she stopped, always right before, like she knew exactly what I was feeling. She moved in front of me and climbed on board, a leg on each side, straddled and ready to go. My lips were buried between her damp braids, sucking on the sweet skin of her neck. She smelled earthy, she radiated warmth. My skin slid into hers, an insane mixture of oil and wet, of sweat breaking through sealed pores, mingling into the slip of our movements.

Then she took it from me again, gone, disappeared. I felt wrung out, sore, overloaded, but relieved. She held me in her slippery embrace, still straddling me.

"Sleep…." Purred into the ear she chewed on.

Razor appeared in the doorway of the intensely

hued dinning room. A pale, thin woman with dark

hair gripped his left arm.

"How good of you to come!" Johnston's bloated

voice boomed. "Please introduce us to your

friend, Doctor."

Gila looked around uneasily, her dark eyes wide

and nervous. She had seen these people before.

She knew what they would do.

A long oval table, dressed with red silk, bled into

the crimson walls. Here sat six, all looking,

sneering, sweating, staring. At the head was

Johnston, immense and dripping. On his right was

Splint, short blonde hair and pink stained eyes, he

smiled at her, lips corrupting the gesture into one

of polluted intent. Gila shivered. To his right was

Slather, greasy and nervous, his eyes kept on the

empty china in front of him. Two women followed

the procession, each with jet black hair, one cut

short, the other long and curling. Twins. The one

with the flowing mane smiled sweetly at Gila,

pretty face, perfect makeup, sparkling hazels

laughed and danced in their sockets. The other

sister stared at Razor, her smirk was dangerous,

dirty, and she winked when he looked her way.

The chair at the other end of the table sat empty,

but next to it sat a hulking mass of a man, dressed

in a buttoned-up white shirt, straight black tie. His

arms seemed to push at the fabric, stretching the

seams. Bald head, shaven clean, rigid posture, his

look was stern and unmovable. Razor took the seat

next to him. He nodded at the skinhead,

"Toulmac."

"Doctor," southern smooth reply.

Gila took the chair next to Razor, Johnston on her other side.

Razor cleared his throat, "This is Gila. My special case."

"Gila?" Splint spoke up, "Like the monster? Like a lizard?" He giggled obnoxiously and leaned across his plate at her.

Gila froze, jaw clenched tight and grinding, hand squeezing Razor's under the table.

Everyone then sat silent, eyes darting, quiet, sneaky signals exchanged, atmosphere tensing. They waited for someone, something...

The quivering moment was then split apart by a moan of wood, a squeal of a hinge. Toulmac stood quickly, expectant of whatever was coming through the doorway.

It seemed the figure suddenly appeared in the room, like some kind of female version of Nosferatu himself. She was tall and painfully thin. White hair pulled back in a bun so tight that it threatened to rip the tissue paper skin around her face. Narrow, hooked nose and sunken, milky eyes were the only noticeable features on her decaying face. The long black dress that hung on her emaciated frame looked priestly, minus the collar. She stood there holding a pale leather book in her withered talon-like hands.

Except for Toulmac, fear was the main expression on everyone's face. Razor was looking down, trying to avoid the old woman's glare.

Johnston managed to remove himself from his chair. "Welcome Mother. Please join us and bless the food we are about to receive."

She turned her blind eyes to him, looking like a giant vulture, cocking her head to one side as she scanned the table. She then opened the pale leather book.

"Bereven serpents," she croaked in a harsh Germanic gurgle, "for you all are going to hell. This food is fodder for your mouths of filth."

Silence coated the room. She glided to the end of the table and took the seat next to the attentive Toulmac. Then she turned her gaze to Splint.

"Don't forget your lessons, pagan. You were not present for last Sunday's teaching."

Toulmac glared at him as he sat down slowly. Splint averted his eyes.

"Sorry, Mother. It won't happen again." Splint looked sick as he mumbled the apology.

The ancient wraith then proceeded to clasp her hands in prayer, her speech turning to German.

"Amen." Rice paper lids parted to reveal the clotted cream stare, slowly rolling to rest upon Gila.

"Doctor, who is this?"

Everyone started to eat, pretending not to listen. Razor froze then inhaled sharply.

"A patient of mine, Mother Hildy."

"She looks like a half breed, a heathen," the words flew out sharp and hateful. "Girl, are you a heathen?"

Gila said nothing, but she shook, keeping her eyes down at all costs, like she was sitting at the same table with Medusa herself.

"I thought so. The devil has your tongue." She cackled and stood, rising like smoke from the table. "If he hasn't yet, he will."

I opened my eyes to the dark, too dark, too quiet. I couldn't feel her anywhere near me. I wasn't sure where I was.

Back in the hotel room, Razor kneels in front of her as she sits on the edge of the bed. Gila looks so worried, hopeless....

"Hailey?"

I ask the darkness, I get no reply.

"I promise I won't be long. I have to go, this is my job now, if I like it or not." Razor held her

hands. "I'll only be in New Orleans for a day at the most. If he doesn't make it through the surgery, I'll be back sooner."

I heard weeping from the shadows, soft, quiet. My eyes were so heavy and I kept hearing their voices, kept seeing those images.

She was alone now, all alone in the hotel room.
Night was coming, she got ready for bed and took the pills that he told her to take. Then a car door slammed outside her room.
She only had a minute, if that....

I was on my hands and knees as I crawled looking for Hailey. The dark pressed in on me, into me. I felt the shadows soak through my skin.

"Hailey!"

I was getting pissed, anger growing, squirming into my brain. I couldn't think straight. I was in two places at once. Not right.

Then I saw her, sitting on the table, looking down on me.

"Come here, Hailey."

Not my voice, not me.

Splint burst through the door, curdled smile smeared across his face.

"Here Lizard, Lizard, Lizard..."

This would be her worst nightmare come true.

I knew what I was seeing, I had seen it all before. As I reached for Hailey, pulling her down to the ground, pressing my weight into her, I kept thinking about what they were about to do. I was

looking forward to watching this again. I *wanted*

to see this again.

"I need this, Hailey."

I saw my shirt laying across the table and I went

for it, bunching it up, started to stuff it into her

mouth.

Gila made muffled noises through the shirt that

choked her, as Splint moved between her legs,

Slather holding her down.

I pushed deep into her, the familiar warmth. I

pinned her arms above her head. This way would

be better, the right way. She needed this as much

as I did. Maybe, I would just pretend she was Gila,

as I closed my eyes and watched the scene play

out inside my head I would do the same thing.
Yes.

Then it all changed.

I felt hard dirt on my cheek and pressure on my arm that was twisted behind my back. Hailey sat on top of me, holding me down, and whispered in my ear, "This has gone too far. This will stop."

She let go of my wrists and grabbed my hair, forcing me up on my knees. The burn was gone and instead I started to feel the stirrings of humiliation sprouting in my cooling brain.

"You've gone too deep, this will not do." She sounded different, her voice was deeper, stern.

She kneeled behind me, her left arm roped around my neck, keeping me in place.

"You think you know what is right. You think this dark thought is the way. I will show you another way."

She forced my head to the wall with the incredible color, the undulating patterns. They were moving, they swirled. My chest tightened, and I tried to close my eyes, but I couldn't. The swirls turned to figures, figures into familiar faces. The hotel room and Gila on the floor, the scene I just woke from. I stared at her still form, tried to remember the smell of her hair.

"Yes, remember how she felt underneath you, the fragrance of her fear."

I did, I put myself right there. It was easy, and the picture seemed to fade, then disappear. I pushed ethics out of my thoughts and went full force. I felt my tongue slide around her ear, tasted her blood. I opened my eyes and saw hers, huge and dark and full of me. I knew this was wrong, I knew. But I wanted to be close to her again, and this was the only way.

"No, Charlie, it is not the only way," and Gila glared up at me through pink stained eyes, words spoken from changing, thinning lips, chin sprouting stubble.

I felt myself flipping over, onto my back, arms forced up and pinned down. Intense pressure filled my chest, disbelief drowned my thoughts.

Splint leered down at me and smiled, rank sweat dripped into my face. I felt pain in between my legs. I went to scream, and found my mouth already open, wide open and filled with *my shirt. I try to call out, to bring Razor back, but I can't.*

Why is this happening? What have I done to deserve this? But I know what I have done, and I do deserve this.

The horrid blonde one is licking my ear, plugging it up and he calls me sickening things, tells me I need this. The panic shocks my head and takes me away from what he does. I look at the ceiling, I count the cracks, but it hurts and it brings me back.

I am sick. I have never been so sick. I cannot believe this is happening, this is not happening. No. No, no, no!

There are pictures in my mind, pretty pictures of Ginger, of Grandpa, of the smooth warm rocks in the sand. I am there and I am safe and happy. Safe and warm.

But the desert is fading into the hopelessness

that soaks me to my very core. I open my eyes to

the blonde one kneeling between my legs. I go to

move, to get away and he holds me down and the

other one comes to help.

New pain rips through me, fresh and

unbearable. My thigh is on fire, the muscles

cramping, tightening, swelling. This is worse than

the pain between my legs. Hot blood is rushing

out, I know, I feel it pooling underneath me, and I

try so hard to fight, to get away, but the strength

leaves me with the blood, running out and over,

going, going...

Before I go, I should say I am so sorry,

Grandpa. I am so sorry I let you die.

I wake up gasping, gulping air like coming up from water.

I open my eyes and find myself bent over Hailey's knees, gagging and coughing. It hurt to breathe. I was in some sad shape.

"Charlie! Charlie, it has passed. Come come, sit up."

What the fuck? This is all I could think, all my brain would let me think. Did that just happen, what I thought just happened?

I was her, right? For a little while, long enough to feel what happened that I couldn't really think about right at the moment. No that would be insane. Just a weird dream, didn't happen.

"Really?" Hailey responded to my thought that she couldn't possibly have known, since I didn't say it out loud. See? Insane.

"What the fuck?" See? All I could think.

"Like I said, Charlie, a different perspective. I brought you to another place, to see in a better way."

My stomach turned inside out as the sensation of being smothered with Splint's body washed over me. There were stabs of pain in places I didn't even possess. Christ, I was going to puke again.

"Why?" I managed to say between the dry heaves, wiping away thin spit threads, trying to pull it together.

She got up, turned her back to me. "Better to be the victim than the victimizer." She was at the wall then, that wall of moving, living color, touching it, caressing it. "There's much more to this story, if you have the strength to know it."

Did I? Good question.

"But I think you need to rest, you are having trouble digesting what I have fed you."

Well, that was a disturbing way of looking at it. I started to puke. Jesus, what did she feed me? My head swam then it throbbed. Wait…was this my head? My thoughts? Who am I? Paranoia seeped in and I swore I could hear his laughter, feel his fingers….

I wanted to run, get away, but I was weak, and I could fell the threat of unconsciousness press in around me, but that fear of what lay behind its black curtain kept turning on the lights, making me jump and snap, electric panic popping inside my burned out brain.

"Settle, be calm and settle." That embrace again, narcotic contentment blanketed me with thick sedation, and it did calm me, settled me.

I dreamt of stupid things, wonderful and empty

of anything weird or important. Of painting, of

walking, of drinking cool, cool water. But then I

dreamt of being really young again, and playing

outside in our yard in Clearwater. The air was

perfect, a breeze you could drink, cool and clear.

The sun warmed the green of the grass, releasing

it, drifting up into my brain, reminding me of all

the summers, of all the drinkable days that I have

ever had. I walked the yard, my bare feet

cushioned by thousands of bending blades, by the

soft, soft dirt.

I looked up to see people on the other side of my

fence, two women, familiar, standing, staring.

They talked to each other and nodded. The one

was older and had wrinkled dark skin and a bright

blue bandanna on her head. The other, she made my stomach flip, made me shake. They waited, it seemed they wouldn't come in. She smiled at me and waved, the one I couldn't stop staring at, the one I knew so well.

I heard my mom inside the house and she was crying, and I knew not to go in, because she would be at that desk again, and she would be bleeding. So, I decided to open the gate, because I had to know, had to find out the rest of the story.

"Prophetic?"

Razor sat in front of Johnston's wide bulk, his shirt bloodied from the surgery, face worn and worried.

"Yes, she has these dreams," he swallowed hard, "sometimes they seem to come true." Razor already regretted having this conversation.

"Please, tell me more." Johnston's impatience stained the air between them. "Can she control it?"

Razor shook his head, "No. But why I'm telling you this is because she dreamt about something that she thinks will happen here at the house."

"Hmm,"

"She thinks, well, an accident of some kind will occur." He should have never had said anything, but maybe if Johnston knows about this, maybe it wouldn't happen.

"Who would this concern?"

"The cook."

"My new cook?"

Razor nodded without looking up.

"Well, Doctor, I would tell your patient not to worry. I'm sure it was just a nightmare."

"A nightmare, this is only a nightmare."

She was laughing as I woke up.

"How ya feelin'?"

My stomach had stopped churning, but I could taste the familiar dead mouse undertones that coated my swollen tongue. "Super."

She sat down next to me, she smelled good, like fresh laundry hanging in the sun.

"Can you think on it now?"

"No, not really."

"Do you need another nap?" She smiled, tricky.

"What do you want me to think?" I know I was still in some sort of denial.

"Did you understand me when I said, better to be the victim than-"

"The victimizer, yes." I tried to think of her then, Gila, and I felt sick. Not that she made me sick, but that I made myself sick. How I had thought of her before, the pain and the control, the pale, anemic images that crawled out of the slimy wrinkles in my brain, this is what made me sick.

"Do not condemn your actions too quickly, learn to accept, understand."

Understand? What did that mean?

I wanted to run away then, get out and start to forget this. But there was something that poked, that wouldn't let me self-indulge. "What did they do to her? What happened next?" To say that, it hurt, it ached. My legs shook with the thought of it, unconsciously preparing myself to make it to the door, to freedom.

But before I could do anything I regretted, I felt her lips on mine. Warm pressure turning to gentle traces of a slick tongue, following cold tracks of dried tears across my cheeks, to rest upon each eyelid, closing them softly with a kiss.

I woke in a car.

I feel different, I feel numb. Then I feel hot, it rushes over my body like flames. I go to move, but I can't. There is something pressing around me, tight, confining.

I start to scream, I can't control it, it just comes, and I don't know what I am going to do, how I can get away. Everything floods back, and I remember what happened to me.

The car stops. There's light because they open

the top and get me out of the trunk. Them again. I

can't do this. I can't focus my eyes, blurry,

everything is moving so fast.

"Why the fuck do we have to bring her here?"

"Shut up. Get her out, bring her downstairs."

"This is fucking crazy."

"She wants to see her, so just fucking do it!"

I can hardly feel anything as they pull me out.

This is a blessing. I am moving through the dark.

They bring me to that house, the death house. I

don't want to go in there.

"Can she even hear us?"

"Who fucking cares."

We go inside. I hear things like wailing,

pleading, things begging for release. I am losing

my grip. I feel my thoughts turning to rushing water. Have to hang on.

Downstairs, many steps deep into the bowels of the death, into the damp dark, blooming with mildew, dressed with vapors of dissected frogs. Then, no more light. I am dying finally.

"Did you bring me die Heidin?"

Angular harshness piercing my head and a dim, dim light fills my thoughts.

"Heidin hear me!"

This brings tears to my eyes, the knives of her voice cut through the numbness and I cry out in pain.

"Do you know where you are? You are in a place for sinners, for whores." Sandpaper laughter.

Whores?

"Heathen, see me!"

My eyes pop open, stretched wide to obey what she has said. I see her now, I see the thinness, her decay. I also see the hate that surrounds her like a cloud. I try to focus on it and it moves in circles, grows darker. Now I can't look away.

"You have something though. Potential. If you live, you may understand."

The cloud-shadow moves up, around and in. It is forming, slowly becoming solid. The numbness in my mind is parting to let a realization through. It reaches me with it's warning. It tells me to close my eyes. Too late.

"Do you see it?" Her words hold surprise at this. "You can see my angel."

No. No angel, this thing that forms, hideous, vile. Black, it oozes from the cloud. Shiny, slippery, filling out, spreading like mold. I try to look away, but it holds me in its stare, heavy, dark, and brimming with insanity. Eyes that want to suck me in, they burn me like the sun.

"Yes! The glory you must see!"

It hovers behind her, shoving its boney hands inside her head, but she doesn't move, why can't she feel this? Then something moves from behind It, unfolding slowly, wings unfurling, torn with holes. Then It smiles at me, the gleaming oil of its face splitting open to reveal sharp spikes of horror, rows upon rows of thin needle teeth.

"Oh yes! The glory! The blessing you witness...you will never forget this!"

I see It move to whisper into her eggshell head and she nods and smiles and whispers back. She says things I can't understand.

"Get on your knees, Heathen, and thank God for what you are about to receive."

She starts to move around me and It follows gliding with her, cloven feet that don't touch the ground. Cloven feet. This is not happening.

"My angel has given me the news and it says to make it separate, to uncoil the potential, to split you in half. I do this to perfect the technique so I can spread the word, to show that the chosen few have the thread of heaven inside, hidden, and I have the divine mission to seek them out and pull it free from believers and heathens alike. Here we make a new race of angels on earth, to remake the garden that man, in his ignorance, has shat upon." Then she comes close, so close that I can smell the death that rides on her words. "Don't be flattered, heathen. You are only an example."

She starts to circle me, and her speech turns different, angular, and hurtful. I can't look away from the disease that follows her. I hear a word. One word that she spits at me, over and over, and it feels like splintered glass. I cover my ears with my hands, but the word bleeds through, burrowing in, swelling and filling my mind. It is horrible. Something cracks inside my skull and it pulls itself from me, leaving a screaming, gaping hole. Pulling, yes, an indescribable pulling. I am being pulled apart.

I am not aware of the pain in my head, only the absence of something that rushed through me, slimy and cold, and I shiver with the touch of it. There is great fear around me, incredible tension. Then I hear a voice. It waivers with sorrow, grows louder with unbearable pain, the screaming fills my ears. I realize that it is coming from my own

lips.

"Amen!"

I look through the spaces of my fingers to see

something hover above me, something red, rolling

forming...

Out of the bloody veil, it pushes through. Wet,

scaly, unclean, and it shines with some kind of

unholy afterbirth. It shines. It turns a reptilian

head to me, and it smiles, mouth packed solid with

jagged shards of bleeding glass. Two holes filled

with dazzling color open slowly to reveal a

dominant shade of green, eyes that glow with

emerald fire, flames that burn with unfathomable

loathing, bottomless madness, hard and scorching,

a sight born from the depths of the darkest

thoughts.

This monster is heavy. It crushes me with the weight of its stare. I feel myself slipping, thoughts thinning, sight leaving....

Hailey was sitting on top of me and there was blood everywhere. I noticed that my nose hurt really bad. Reason tells me not to think about it too much, it's better I didn't know.

"Charlie, Charlie, it's over, it's done." She kept repeating that, I could hear a degree of concern in her words.

"What happened? What was that?" I asked, feeling a hot, salty glob of clotted blood slide down my throat. That image of what hovered above Gila lurked behind my lids, I didn't want to close them, didn't want to see that again ever again.

She rolled off of me, pushed me up, and took my face between her soft hands. "Are you with me?"

"What?"

"Are you here with me?"

I shook my head and it throbbed. I looked at her and asked the same question. Was I? No answer.

"What was that? What did Johnston's mother do to her?"

Hailey looked down, deep in thought, "She is a story onto herself," she got up and went to the wall of color, touching it gently. "Hildy, in her arrogance, believed that she herself was blessed with an angel, one that came from inside her own soul." Hailey shook her head, "That could never happen. The only things in our souls are things that need to be washed clean and understood. Only then can we transcend our flesh." The colors seemed to move under her hand. "Hildy was tied with the darkest forces that are. They showed her the way to make manifest the filthiest parts of one's totality. To allow the aspects of hell in one's soul to become an entity, a creature apart from its creator."

All this was making my head spin even more. "But why her? Why do this to Gila?"

She stepped away from the wall and looked at me, "Because Gila had something wounded in her that called out to be seen. Shouted out to anything that would listen. Many have a darkness that overruns and controls one's actions. No proper balance and that leads to harsh condemning of one's own being. She believed she deserved all that happened to her. When you give something that much power, it starts to run the show."

I felt like crying. It seemed this story was just so sad, that nothing could save her from this. Now she was chained to a bed, locked away in an attic.

"Don't give up on her yet. Gila is one who walks with the medicine, some say. The way of one who travels this path comes to many a roadblock, many forks in the road but she has many outside of this world who would guide and keep close eye on her." Hailey's eyes narrowed into slits, focusing her intent onto my face, "She has much power, Charlie."

I couldn't quite follow her, what her words meant exactly. I started to doubt that this was really going on at all.

"Come over here," she led me to a blanket on the floor. "Lie down for awhile, rest."

I did, but there was no way I was going to sleep.

I wasn't falling for that one again, lady.

Famous last words.

There was dust under my hands, in my mouth. I open my eyes to purple light melting into the clear of the day. On a road all alone. Where am I?

I go to get up, I want to rise, but it does not happen. Why? My leg is heavy and full of pain, red and crusted with....

I can't breathe, can't catch my breath, suffocating, choking. Help me! Someone! Where am I? What is happening?

Far away, I can hear something. I look around and see empty fields, rusted things, a dead mill, and silent factories. I am in a wasted place, and now I identify the sound of barking dogs.

This will have to wait. I need to know why my leg is bad, why I am here. But the barking is closer now, and I remember something about dogs running wild, about no fear and viciousness. I need to move. Bushes near the dust. I drag myself there. I should be quiet and....

He said I needed this. Who? Why is the fear coming? Why is my chest filling with tightness? He called me things, he came in and they held me down. No, that was just a nightmare. Stop crying. Have to find a phone, got to call Razor.

I see them. I see a skinny black dog and he bristles with distrust. He growls and walks slow up to the bushes. He smells the ground that I passed over, smells the blood I have left behind.

That dream I had, basements and dissected frogs. Something there, something red and shining.

Don't look him in the eye, Grandpa told me that. I still hear his growl. I look down at my leg. There was a knife in my leg. He pushed it through and I felt my blood leaving. THAT was the dream, and this is a dream.

Now I see the others coming. Some are small, some hairy and dirty. They all approach slowly, they come to find the source of the blood. Must be hungry. I wonder if they will eat me, I laugh. The black one is poking his muzzle through, close to my leg. I can see his long teeth.

A horrible croaking voice is filling my head, 'Threads of heaven, pull them free.' What is that? Who was that? I must be sleeping, still dreaming.

The black dog is gone, and I hear a rumble of growls, snapping of teeth. I look up and see her, a swollen yellow girl, and she stands in the middle of the pack. She looks like Ginger. This one I look in the eyes. She knows, and she comes waddling up, tail wagging slow into the bushes. I can touch her head, and feel her tongue. She claims me as one of her own. She must be Ginger, in all of my dreams it's Ginger.

Something left me, something is gone. It lurks outside, around and, unfound. What could this be?

Her fur is dirty and dry. She is dusty, just like me. Her belly is stretched tight, like she will pop soon. I wonder how many puppies she will have. I feel shaky, tired. I don't feel right. There's pain going up my left side, red spreading upward, boiling like water. Boiling like blood. And it pokes through, shining with some kind of unholy

afterbirth, it shines....

"No,"

"Here, Lizard, Lizard, Lizard."

I don't think I can do this. I think I will just rub

her behind the ears, she seems to like that. Maybe

I'll name her Ginger.

The tears come down like rain and they soak

into her fur. I'm not strong, and I hope I die

before all the bad things come through. It's hard

to hold things back. My body pleads for sleep, but

I curse it, hate it, but need it.

But there is no comfort here. Cold coated panic,

images coming through, things I will disown and

say never happened. I hear Razor. He's here, I

feel him, his pain, the thickness in his words,

suffering in his throat. Why? The pain in my thigh

is on fire, and it burns through the denial of my

thoughts, burns me to the bone. I think I need to

call to my grandfather before I go, call in the old

tongue, so he will understand me. Tell him that his

granddaughter is weak, sick, and dying. Forgive

me. Give me safe passage. But something heavy

holds me down. Something red and shiny and

familiar. One word spat out like cancer, seeping in

like ice to spread open the fissures, cracking free

the thread that she would pull out. Make separate.

My hand goes out to touch Ginger's soft fur, to

give me some small comfort as I wait for death,

but instead it feels like cold skin, supple but

chilled. I open my eyes to something that shines,

something almost too bright to be seen and it hurts

to look at it. Something is kneeling next to me and

I can see her face, it's distorted but not in anger

or pain but in deformity. She is twisted and bent all over, pink scars puff out from her flesh and she is missing her arm. Who is this? My heart starts to hurt with her presence and I want to reach out to help her. Her face is stillness, reminding me of my grandfather's. She has a small smile on her crooked lips. Maybe she is here to take me to him.

"This will pass, Gila. First step taken." A young voice, soft, quiet.

I want to cry, not for me but for her. I go to reach out, to touch her round caved-in face, and that's when I see a small tattered wing, hanging limp from her broken back. What is this? My mind is spinning again, I can't hold on to this reality much longer. I think I will sleep for awhile. Maybe this is when I will finally die.

"Hello," heavy word spoken softly.

I open my eyes not to the mangled angel-thing,

but to a man in a stained army coat. Dirty face,

tangled light hair. Blue eyes that float and that

keep me awake.

"She looks like she's been hurt, Mama." My

yellow dog looks up, tail wagging for him too.

Who is this and why am I here?

"Her leg is bad but can be fixed."

His voice feels like warm water, it brings the

tears so close, but I won't. No. Something wants to

open up, someone wants to hold her arms out for

him to take her home. Tell me who I am.

"Can I help you?"

It swells in me, it seems to come out of my eyes,

the want of it. I will not say it. I will not ask for

help. He stares at me for a long, long time. I don't

know him. He might hurt me, just like the blonde

one. So I stare back and say nothing. I am nothing. Yellow girl whines low in her throat and she puts her weight up against me. She keeps me safe. The dirty man just smiles.

"She likes you," whisper thin, "she's been waiting for you."

Waiting for me? How long? I touched her back, boney and long. How long?

"My name is Sibby. What's yours?"

Name? I don't want to know my name. I don't want to dig that deep. I'll just sit here with Ginger until I wake up.

I feel something heavy leaning on my shoulder, I turn but nothing is there. I don't know what to do, I don't know...

"Why don't you close your eyes, rest a little, " his voice coats me in warm thickness, soft touches.

I fight to keep my eyes open but they won't. I feel the familiar sinking, rushing of hot color. I know I'm sleeping, but it seems different, more coherent. I have an overwhelming feeling to run, to get out before anything happens.

I hear a voice from far away, "Someone is knocking on your door, Little one. Go see who it is."

I turn to see it, a massive wooden door, and instantly it shakes with the want of fists on the other side. Do I really want to open it?

I reach for the silver knob, cold in my grasp, pain coming into my arm, down my leg. So much of it, too much to feel. The door opens. It swings wide, violent and impatient. I jump aside. My eyes fall upon a figure in the doorway. I won't have this, not happening.

"Lover," It gurgles and smiles. It smiles.

I go to run, to get away. God, please help me,
please, please, please.

I'm grabbed from behind, my shoulder aches
with its touch. It forces me around and I look into
that wound of a face, those impossible green eyes.
Please don't smile again. I gag with the sight, the
grin opening like a demonic flower, raw and
ripped, dripping with bloodied gore, the shards in
its mouth glinting, reflecting back my face a
thousand times.

"Lover submit," like a noise from the grave, dirt
filled and decaying. I squirm from its grip,
running, running. Another door, another room,
and I see myself on the floor, held down and
gagged, blood oozing from my leg. I turn away
and run some more, out of there, into here, a cold

place, the air dark and stained with the deaths of frogs. The old hag turns to face me, harsh words flinging out to wound me, tearing me in half. My head hurts horribly and I fall to the cement, screaming, wanting this to end, never have I wanted something so badly...

The noise and pain suddenly disappear, replaced by intense cold. I open my eyes to a frost smothered place, the same place, but clean and quiet. So quiet. Beautifully quiet.

I look around to find the horror, to see if It has followed me, and I see It, standing frozen and still, the thin ice covering It stained pink with blood.

I know now a little of what has happened. But I don't know why. The cold is being filled with a sound, a voice, and I feel my screams rush from my throat, burning my flesh like fire.

"Wake up, Little one," I follow Sibby's words out of my insanity. I wake up into my nightmare.

"Do you know what this thing is?"

I try to ignore him and poke at the fire.

"Well I know. It's your darkness, your pain, your fear, and definitely your anger."

"You still think this is from me? I think she pulled it out of hell, I know she did."

He stirs his beans over the fire, "Yes, she did. Out of your hell. This is all yours, Little one."

I look down at my leg and see the scab. I touch it, feeling the way it dips into my flesh. It still hurts. I press harder.

"How's the leg?"

"Fine."

"So, do you understand? Are you even listening to me?"

"Understand what?" I've lost my patience. "That I'm fucked? Yeah, I understand. Why is that so important to you?" I don't want to think about It, I don't want to wake it up.

"You're not fucked, and quit swearing so much. If you really understood what I said, you would know that this is a part of you, and if you accepted that, I could help you out a little bit better," he doesn't even look up, just sits there, poking at the little pot.

'Liar!' In my head I hear this. My stomach sinks, I don't want this, please go away.

"You must accept this, you must embrace this cancer, love it as your own. This is the only way to control it." Sibby looks up, and he knows It *whispers in my head, he always does. "Look it in the eye. Then you can bring it back, absorb and integrate, be one again."*

Unbelievable. What a load of shit. The anger rises like muddy water. 'Why don't you tell him? Tell him how much you hate him, how you would like to kill him in his sleep.' I hear the hateful murmurs dribble out like sewage.

"Why don't you talk to me, Little one?" And he gives me that look, like he knows what I'm thinking.

"I think you're full of shit, Sibby." I blurt out. "You have no answers, never did." The mud is clouding my sight, blurring the light in his eyes.

"Did it tell you to say that?" His voice always so fucking calm.

"Go to hell, old man! I never asked for any of this!" Rooms in my head being filled, growing heavy with the heat....

"Those aren't your words, I don't believe you, Gila."

This one word, it clears my mind, doors shutting, mud draining away. "What did you say?" For days I have been here, listening to Sibby's words, letting him heal me, teach me, and never once did I tell him that, never did I say that word, that name.

"I said I don't believe you," small smile spreads, "Gila."

"How do you know that?"

"What? That your real name is Gila? The name your grandfather gave you? How do I know?" He gets up and walks over to sit on a dirty block of

concrete, *"Your grandfather came to me some time ago, told me of your dilemma."*

I choke on my surprise, "What?" I can barely whisper, "I don't..."

"He did. You should know better than that, Gila. You know what he is, what he can do."

"No, he can't come back from the dead, that's impossible! You never knew him, this is just another one of your fucking tricks!"

"Oh yeah?" His voice goes cold. "You think you know it all, don't you, Little one? Think you could've saved everything, changed everything, don't you? You couldn't. You may have dreamt his death, but you couldn't prevent it. He knew, Gila. You could've told him about the red Chevy pickup, about the hick that was driving it. Hell, you could've even told him why that redneck had it out

for Indians, but it wouldn't have mattered! He

knew it too. He knew he was going to die."

How does he know this? How can I believe him?

"He showed me everything," Sibby whispered,

taking my hand, squeezing it, "I saw what

happened to you. He asked me to help, he told me

you would be coming."

How did he know about the truck that killed my

grandfather? Something says that I should know

better. How can this be possible? But then again,

how can something red and hideous that was

chanted out of my soul be possible?

Back in the desert with him, when I was so

small, my grandfather would lift me up onto the

big, smooth rocks to tell me all the stories, all the

lessons.

"One day you will become a healer, one who walks with the medicine," I believed that too, until I learned the story of my mother, the sad song of my beginning, the truth of Razor. Then I pulled it apart, all that hope and faith. I put it away, deep down in the dark, never to touch that thought again.

"You are sad. It stains you to your very core." Sibby and his bath water words, making me so heavy. "You have a gift, I know you don't want to hear that, but you do. Let me help you."

Unbelievable.

"A gift? Come on, Sib. It's far from it."

I sit in the dust, remembering everything. My grandfather always said that it was a gift to dream the way I do, to walk what hasn't been traveled yet. To see things before they happened, to know

when and where, but never why.

The first dream I ever had like that was when

Ginger would die, how I would find her, torn and

bloated in the sand, believing it was just a

nightmare, I did nothing. She disappeared and

that was when the first sprout of doubt pushed

through, telling me that I should have listened.

Now I would be sorry. I sat in the sand, watching

the flies crawling in and out of the gashes in her

stomach, knowing that this was my fault.

What would it matter anyway? These days I

have something worse to worry about.

'You're fucked, anyway you look at it, you're

fucked,' It whispers, a rushing sound of

hopelessness, and I know I will never get away

from this. I feel my body curling, face in between my knees. Safer here, smaller.

I feel Sib's hand on my back, moving up to my neck, "But first we need to tame this monkey of yours," he lays down next to me in the dirt, wrapping himself around the ball of my body. "Close your eyes, just for a little while. I'll keep you safe."

His words burn into my brain. I push myself up, turn over, and look at him.

"What do you mean, 'tame my monkey'?"

He smiles up at me, "I mean control it, you know, make it cold."

"Cold?"

He rolls onto his back, looking up into the sky, searching for the words. "You have to be really quiet to be cold. You have to be still," whispered

into the air.

He confuses me, I don't know what to think.

"Who are you, Sib?" Because I really don't

know.

"Just a man," looking down at his feet, "I was a

lot like you, lost, sad. I was once separate too, but

I was born that way. I had voices, had visions,"

small laughter. "The doctors, well, they had many

a name for it, lots of theories, lots of pills. Nothing

worked, so I went away and came here. I was

alone with my voices and I learned that there is no

two, there is only one." Looking into my face,

tears close to the rim of his blues, "I learned that

the sickness was a part of me, caused by me. I

accepted this. I submitted to my weakness and that

allowed me to shine light upon it, to truly see it

and in doing that I became at peace, I swallowed it whole." His eyes glow in the fading light of the day. "No two, Gila. Only one."

He grabs my hand.

"I became silent inside. Balanced and sometimes cold."

"I don't think I could ever be silent inside, Sib."

"I think you can," he says, sitting up. "But you have to understand that this is you, Gila. All that hate and dark, it's yours."

Sibby looks at me in a way that pierces me to the bone, in a way that takes all my secrets and lays them dead and splayed upon the cracked asphalt.

"No, I can't believe that," my voice cracks with the fear. "This thing, it was put into me, I'm cursed, Sib! It was chanted out of hell! Why can't you understand that?"

"Oh, I do," his look going dark. "Chanted out of your hell. This is your darkness, all your poisons, collected into this stalking shadow."

I can't listen to this. I get up, my legs shaky, weak. Where am I gonna go?

'Just end it,' It whispers, 'it's all just a silly game anyway. Climb the beams, until you're really high up, then jump,' telling me this like a friend sharing secrets through a cupped hand. My heart skips, stomach twisting into hard knots. What am I thinking?

I hear Sibby's voice from behind me, "This darkness, it will first beg at your table to then steal the food right from underneath your nose. This is how it will devour you, tricking you in your denial, and then you will start to wonder how you have become so thin."

I bolt from him and run as fast as I can. Maybe I
will run so fast that the darkness won't know
where I went. I will lose myself in the speed, leave
that part behind in the wind. I run until I fall,
nothing left, no resistance, no panic, too tired. I
close my eyes in a patch of tall grass. I can feel
sleep circle me like a feral dog; mangy, thin, teeth
barred.

I bow my head to my rabid gift, I hope it eats me
alive.

"Charlie?"

Her voice seemed to form patterns in the thick shadows of the room. I kept still, watching them, the way they bounced off the walls, multiplied, echoed.

"Charlie!"

That one hurt my ears. I should get up.

She was looking at me in this weird way, it concerned me, made me nervous.

"The night grows thin, Charlie. It may be time for you to go," she said in a too quiet way, a cautious way.

"Why?" I didn't want to go yet. I was getting used to this sleep, wake up, sex thing.

She came around to me, touching me with those warm, soft hands, sending shivers radiating through my skin. The want of her resounded back three fold. I needed her again.

"There may not be time," breathy sweet in my ear, and I thought to myself, there's always time.

This time I was with her, not Gila. I know Gila in ways that would prevent me from doing those things to her anymore. Well, not here anyway.

Towards the end, she had me on my back, riding me hard, sweat dripping from her face, into mine. I could taste it on my lips, feel it in my eyes. I was close, and it was an intense mix of pleasure and bliss. The soreness of my body added to the confusion, muscles suffering with the urgency of my movements, rushing towards the inevitable spill, the unbearable pull….

"Charlie, it's time to go."

My mind was racing, wait, there was something I needed to ask, what was it? She stood there, looking down at me and I felt so small. But there were things I needed to know before she kicked me to the curb.

"So that's it? That's all you're going to show me?" A little reverse psychology never hurt.

She didn't say anything. It wasn't working.

"But what about Sibby? About what he taught her, what did he teach her? You can't leave me hanging like this." I was pleading to a hard, unmoving statue of a creature.

She was shaking her head, a small smile appearing from underneath the thin braids.

"One more, that is all."

I have been here too long.

Under my skin, something itches, something telling me I have to go.

"I know about birds flying south, Lizard," he says softly. I will miss him. I know he still has much to say about the nature of my beast, what I should do, how to do it. I know too, Sibby.

Today I sit and listen to the sluggish water gurgle in its ditch, cottonwood floating and slowing in the clear air. Not all of his words have been wasted on me though, I have learned how to be still, how to freeze my thoughts, make them silent and cold. He tells me that I'm missing the point, but I don't care. I'm finally quiet inside.

But today is different, because I've been dreaming again. The rabid dog has shown me things that kill the quiet, make me afraid.

"Sib?"

He watches the cottonwood too. It seems to amuse him, "What?"

"I've been dreaming."

He turns his head to my voice and rolls his bright blues to me, "I know. You've been crying in your sleep." Attention back to the fuzzy snow. "What about, or should I ask, whom?"

I can't say his name, it won't come out. I wonder if he's real, if I dreamt him up, all the memories fake, hallucinations. But his face is there, pale and thin, his dark hair longer now. How long has it been?

"You say things in your sleep. You say, 'Razor'."

I can't stop the pain now, it comes out heavy and wet, pathetic and weak. "I know he's not well. He screams in these dreams, he suffers...." I know he's looking at me with pity. I wish he would watch the snow.

"Are you sure of this?"

I can't answer him. I can only see Razor's twisted face. He's making quick and painful movements, fingers slipping with the blood as the

239

blade rips across his skin, skin already scarred and beaten.

"I think I need to show you one more thing before you leave me." Heavy hand on my shoulder. "You're gonna learn how to collar that mongrel, make it work for its keep."

"What?"

He smiles and shakes his head, "Learn how to dream. This gift of yours, learn how to use it."

He sits across from me, the fire in between. He has been quiet for too long, and now it's dark and I jump at the slightest noise.

"Are you ready?"

My heart pounds through my chest. "Yes."

"I am going to show you how to run with it, how to jump the void, into his head."

"Wait... into his thoughts?"

"Yes, his thoughts, now pay attention." He gets up and grabs his blankets, making his bed next to the fire. *"Can you go back into that dream, the one you've been having about him?"*

"Yeah, I think so. I've been having it every night."

"Good. Will he be sleeping the same time you will?"

"I don't know. Maybe."

"He'll have to be for you to get in. Remember, you are in a dream, you can do these things. Just keep telling yourself that it's only a dream. Right?" He lays down, pulling the blankets over him, gets comfortable, closes his eyes.

Then nothing. Then snoring.

"Wait, that's it?" Unbelievable.

"What do you want? You're the dreamer, not me." He rolls over, leaving me alone.

I listen to him snore for awhile, then I think about lighting his blanket on fire. I'm tired and as I lay by the popping flames I wait for the cur to circle, my eyes getting heavy, thoughts scrambling, floating images appear and fade. Then I see the barred teeth, and I wonder if I can run as fast.

I focus on his face, looking into his dark eyes. I call out his name in sleep soaked thickness....

Cold. Intense and sharp, needle thin sensation inserted through my chilled skin. Why am I so cold? I keep walking, the snow deeper in places, sometimes replaced by thick expanses of ice. I walk naked through this winter. I know this place....

The ice groans under my feet and they burn on the cracking, shifting freeze. Its clarity splinters as something comes through. A head, a wet mop of gray hair, a wrinkled face birthed from the womb of this barren place, he raises himself up through the cold, and my grandfather says, "Gila, you are so cold. Why are you so cold?"

"Because I am so tired."

He shakes his head, "You are too afraid. You know that this winter is your own. Warm up, Gila. Do not be afraid of yourself."

I smile to say of course, I know, but I don't.

"Hear me, Gila! A lizard needs sun. No more fear, no more apologies. Warm up!"

Then he's gone, and I stand in a different place, a cold cave full of motionless figures. Around my

shoulders is an old Navajo blanket, and I feel a
little warmer.

I should've told him I miss him. I should've said
more. Why didn't I?

This place, I don't want to be here. It's
dangerous. I should leave now, get away. I look at
the figures, some I know instantly, some forcefully
forgotten. I know the reason for this, it's the way I
learned from Sibby, the way of the cold. They
can't hurt me this way, all frozen still. Never
again.

Something gleams in the corner, something
bleeds. Don't go over there, I don't need to see It
that badly, but I'm coming closer. It stands frozen,
its diseased smile still on its malformed face, its
reptilian face, lizard-like face. I notice movement
at its feet, a pool of thick red slowly spreading

around its clawed toes, warming, thawing slowly.

This shouldn't happen, but it's so hard to keep It

from laughing.

I turn and run, past the slushy demon, past my

screaming mother, past the heavy glare of our

father, past them all right into the bright heat of

the desert.

This scene I will know forever....

Razor slumped in the sand, burned pink and

unconscious. It's so hot, he's so hot, way too hot. I

should go to him. I sit in the sand with him,

shaking and remembering the hallucinations of the

peyote, watch the visions shimmer and dance with

the waves of heat. I gather him up, touching

seared skin, taking him close, rocking slowly with

the intent of protection.

"I will take your water, Razor. I will shield you from the sun."

I do this because I know him, really know him, know him better than I know myself. My other half.

One of the visions grows large, glows bright with blood. No. You are frozen.

"Your stillness shakes with summer sun, Lizard. Your ice can not survive the push of fear, my hand of truth." It stands before me, gurgling through its fractured smile, reaching out a hateful talon. "Why waste time on a dead man? You make a fool of yourself with this display of sentimental memory. You need to be shown the folly of your ways."

An instant, this is all it took for It to wrench him out of my arms. I watch paralyzed as It takes long spikes of fingers to stab into his head, wiggling

deep to scramble his brains.

I feel something unfurl in my gut, moving in

unison with a shadow that has stepped out of a

crease in my mind, an understanding. A flame

rises through the paralysis, casting its light on the

monster before me. This will not happen. It will

not touch these parts, parts still tender and naked

in the gleaming fissures of my memory. It will not.

I stand up to meet its height. I see It for what it

is, and I recognize the face, the same that has

haunted me all my life. All my ghosts, all the

monsters under my bed. This is the thing that has

always whispered the advice to walk away, don't

try, you'll be sorry. How It has grown. The voice

the same. All its advice undermining the

confidence, strengthening the insecurities that

grew like weeds.

I know the anger is growing. How stupid I was

to look away, to freeze it with denial.

"Put him down," my voice clear and loud in the

sunshine, my sunshine.

It turns its hateful lanterns to rest upon my face.

"Angry are you?" Dirt filled laughter. "You better

have a lot of it to be able to fight me, Lizard."

I rip Razor from its grip and I run, not in fear

but in haste. Something I forgot to do, why I came.

Razor fades from my arms, the memory leaving as

I look upon a different place, a line in the sand

growing blurred with the smell of damp, the color

of metal.

As I run, I remember the words of someone

close, but I can't see his face. He said It was a

part of me, but I missed the point. This thing, is it a part, a piece, or is it a disease? Something that needs to be cut out?

I come closer to the shadowy place. I can see inside, it's so different, alien. This is not a part of me. Wet air rushes at me, the smell of steel and damp concrete. This line is huge and deep, like a canyon, and I have to get across. I know something is behind me, and I hear the words coming from far away, "You'll never make it, better turn back now!"

I jump. Intense joy fills my chest, rinsing the fear from my gut. I land lightly on the other side.

But joy quickly fades.

I find myself inside a morgue. Bone chilling damp, evil fumes of embalming fluid, strange perfume of decomposition. Why am I here?

I walk around the steel tables dressed with death shrouds, stiff figures hinted at underneath dingy white sheets, toes poking out from the edges of the cloth. I hear a whisper of movement and I peer over one of the tables to see the sound. My heart sinks with the sight of Razor leaning against the cinderblock wall, sitting in his gleaming pool of blackening blood. I watch him, I stare at his too pale face, listening to soft suffering leaving his blue tinged lips.

"Razor?"

His eyes flutter upward, seeing me he startles, his expression turns to panic and fear.

"Razor, it's me," I come around the table towards him, his eyes huge and unbelieving.

"Gila? You're here. I must be dead now," slurred and weak, he is closing his eyes again.

"Raze, look at me, I'm here."

He opens them with great effort, so heavy with so much pain, "I'm so sorry I let you die. Forgive me." I look down at his hands and see them drenched in darkness, upward slits flaying his wrists open like gutted fish. No, he didn't do this. Please don't let this be happening. His eyes sink shut again.

"No! See me!"

When he opens his eyes this time, he is hardly in them. He is so close...

"I let them get you. My fault." He lifts his hand and a rush of blood follows the movement, falling in his lap. "Remember the desert? It shattered us. I see now. See everything. But too late, Gila."

"What? What do you mean? Why did you do this?" He is fading from me, dying right before my eyes.

"I had to. I wanted to be with you. Rest here with me."

It hurt so much to look at him, knowing what he had just done. What can I do?

"Told you."

I turn to see It here, gleaming wet and bright in this gloom. "I knew this would happen. I know these things, call it a gift."

And It snarls at me like a mongrel dog.

Everything is leaving me, this is too much to carry. Maybe I should slit my wrists too, die with the one thing in my shit- filled life that shined, that mattered. I will submit because this has become too hard, too much.

"That would be easy, Lizard. Then the ones who caused all this will get away unpunished. Don't you want vengeance? Power?" It whispers in my ear, "Do you forget the one who spread you wide, the one who filled you up with his hate?" I shake my head trying to clear it of those poisonous pictures. Don't let them come....

Too late. The images have taken root, and I remember him, the blonde one, Splint. The shame comes thick and suffocating. I crumple with the weight of it. I see the wrinkled face of the old hag, her awful sharp words, the one word, and the one who caused all this. The opportunist who took advantage of Razor, put him in chains of fear and intimidation and the whole fucked up family that slurps up lust and blood like starving hyenas.

I look at Razor. Will he understand? If I could wake him up, will he agree? This is not our fault, this has been done to us, everything taken away. It makes sense, why didn't I see it before? There is anger here now, filling up the spaces in between....

I turn to the hateful part of myself and grab It around its throat, backing It against the wall. "I see everything, demon. I see the wisdom in your words and I also see your fear that my death would create." I squeeze harder. "You really don't want to die, do you? It doesn't matter to me anymore, I have nothing after he's dead. In fact, I think today is a good day to die," and It seems to shiver and dull in brightness. In its eyes I can see the cogs spinning, quickly thinking of something to do, to get me under its thumb again. "Is there anything in your infinite wisdom that can help

him?" My fingers sink in between the slimy scales

of its neck, "Because I can feel the death of my

fear coming close, monster, and soon you will

starve."

Then something flashes in my mind, something

not understood at first. I have a choice. I can die

or I can burn in our vengeance. Why not? We're

almost dead anyway. I will make Razor see, make

him strong, something that he never was.

It begins to move the deformed yawn of its jaws,

"A trade, for an agreement, an understanding,"

its green tinged with desperation, "I can see far, I

can see through. Let me live inside on the fire that

grows in your shadows. This I can eat too, and I

can give you strength, give you power through

your hate."

I raise my other hand towards the demon's face. I touch hard skin, mottled and sharp. In an instant, I feel complete. I understand its purpose, why It stands in my mind. I didn't want to live long, only long enough to kill them all, one by one. We will make this our life's work, this will give us purpose.

An idea is birthed as I take my grip away from its neck, "You should know I could never trust you. No deals, demon. Instead I have one of my own; you will do what you are told, make yourself useful, and maybe, just maybe I might throw you a bone." It stays still, frozen with my intent, as I plunge both hands into its head, digging at each emerald ember until they slide into my sweaty palms. I leave It hanging in the air as I turn back to Razor, now so cold, hardly breathing.

"You will see again, and we will start over,

Razor," I whisper into his ear, laying the green

furies in his blood soaked lap, as I pry open each

limp lid, to scoop out each useless eye, throwing

them at the demon to bounce off its frozen form. I

take a glowing orb and slip it in, again on the

other side.

"Wake up…" My mind is burning, buzzing with

all the new discoveries, incredible possibilities.

This will work. We will be healed through this,

make us whole. Never will we be cold again.

He suddenly jerks, hands flinging up to his face,

clawing at his new eyes. I hold him down, arms

pinned to his side as he screams, eyes opened so

wide. I wonder what he sees, if everything is

different. His face is changing, the look of sadness

replaced by a strange hue of anger. It suits him well.

I reach down for his wrists and find them wrapped with white cloth. He feels warmer, his pale face flushing red. But this is only a dream. I can't heal him through sleep alone. If he really slit his wrists I need to find him, to save him or this will be all for nothing.

"He's been taken care of," a different voice. I turn to see Sibby standing in the shadows, staring at the sightless monster.

"What?"

"It's time to wake up, Little one," a look of disappointment soaking into his weathered face. "I think you've collared the wrong mongrel."

After that I heard a fast noise, like a deck of cards being shuffled, or maybe it was the sound of scratching, tapping claws, running quick and slippery over polished wood.

Whatever it was, I saw things that matched the sounds, blurry at first, then glimpses of simple images like little stories caught in the frame of a view-finder.

A coyote running smooth through a strange house.

Snake eyes flashing dark gold.

Bright blood soaking into the pale pores of an alabaster floor.

Shiny black rubber.

A small mountain of bottle green glass.

Violet irises peeking out from deep wrinkles of purple-black skin.

Then it went silent, black, and cold. Slowly I opened my eyes into Gila again, something telling me that my time was running out.

"I could go in there, you know, and just slit his throat. That would be so much easier than this," Razor breathes into my ear.

I turn and look out the window, going over everything, knowing what we must do.

"We're almost there," Riggs growls, looking back at us over the headrest. I smile at him, he smiles back wider.

I glance around the dark red of the car's interior. It reminds me of blood.

"Johnston's gonna be one sorry son of a bitch when he sees you, Razor," Riggs laughs, filling the car with smooth sound.

We stop and I look out. I see it for the first time

in so many years. That house, death house, I

called it once. It seems like a thousand years ago.

Riggs gets out, walks up to the white pillars, and

slips inside. We wait. I turn to Razor. I know he's

reluctant. I know his heart, know what he really

wants.

"He's not ours to take. He belongs to someone

else." I give him these words, hoping he hears

them.

"I know." He looks at me, anger dancing in the

green. "But we've come so far, we can finish it

here, tonight. Take the rest of them."

I agree. I want this too. But that time had

passed, we have become different, changed. This

cannot be our way any longer.

"No," I breathe into his face, a soft offering of comfort to soothe his fire.

Heavy sigh and shakes his head, picks up my hand and brings it to his lips, "Your wish is my command." I feel his hot kiss brand my skin, and in this moment I know we can never fail.

I see movement from the house, Riggs coming down the steps, back into the car. He sticks his head through the open window, "Let's go. The boss man doesn't buy that I have his long lost Doctor in the car. Maybe I should tell him that me and Sugar raised you from the dead, he might believe that one better."

Razor opens the door, and we get out, walking over pale gravel, walking through pale pillars, through the open door, into the death. A thin pale man leads us up the stairs, and he stares at Razor, unbelieving or not remembering, but still staring.

I watch them go into the office. I hear the pig say Razor's name, the surprise in his voice. I don't go inside instead I walk further down the hall to a closed door to the room I want. I open it, go in.

Dark and musty, the close, thick air pushes against me and I smell him. I can smell him.

I feel my throat tighten, the fear rushing up like vomit. I let the emotion consume and cover me. I feel him inside my body, polluting, infecting. I want to run and hide. I close my eyes only to see his, ugly and cruel, staring back, too close to my face. I remember how I screamed, how I pleaded, how I cried. I will never forget. I stand here shaking, pathetic and weak. My leg has started to throb, the scarred aftermath beginning to remember, physical memory from muscle, it still weeps, suffers.

I breathe deep, washing the emotion with calm, with control. But I am not calm. The fear has solidified to hate, the rough burn of anger. I want this, to swim in the darkness, consumed by the scalding mud. I want to remember all the ways I planned to hurt him, all the ways to make him scream. I smile with the power, it comes to my lips like a hungry whore.

Splint.

"Splint." I say it out loud and my hair stands on end.

I walk around his room, looking at the clutter of clothes and magazines on the floor. I inhale deep, filling my nose with him, becoming intimate, knowing him when he doesn't know. This can be *the exciting part, but not the reason I came. I must*

focus on that reason.

I walk to his closet. I see all his books, all the

bad, bad things he knows. A baseball bat on the

top shelf, I knew it would be there, and I take it

down, heavy and smooth. I walk back to the door

and stand behind it, and I wait for him to come

through.

As I stand here, I think back to the pain. I have

moved it since then, it's not in an important place

in my thoughts anymore, but it does take up space.

The taste is sour rust, the feel of it is damp hot. I

let it form in my mind, the shape is round and

rough, hard and sharp. Sibby taught me this.

I close my eyes and look inside, searching for

these things that I put away, buried deep, but still

shallow enough to find. Here in a swampy place,

green and thick with dark, warm mud, I find the wells, the holes that contain everything. I kneel in the muck, shoving my hands down inside the steaming, tight openings. I bring out handfuls of dirt, and as soon as I throw them to the side, they turn to screams and they grow legs and walk. The voices, the images almost overpower and I almost give into the feeling. They wrap their needy hands around my neck and plead with me to stay, to talk, to take them with me.

Outside of this, I breathe deep. I become aware of the stale air of the room, remind myself of the thing I came here to do. We have become different, I have changed.

Inside, I shove my hands deeper beneath the earth, and I feel my fingers scrape something hard, rough, and sharp. I pull it out and look at

the pain that I have carried, the hate that he

poured over me that soaked into each and every

pore. This is what I have come for and I open my

eyes.

I hear the knob turn, I hear him swear under his

breath as he walks into the room. I see the back of

his blonde head, the hair still short and I let him

close the door before I move, before I raise the

bat.

In the back, dark part of my mind, something is

running. I brace myself for the weight upon my

back, the greedy, hot claws grasping my

shoulders. I feel It pushing in, like the tight fit of a

glove, as It slides its own ruin of a face into my

head, penetrating my mind and eyes, wearing me

like a mask. Instantly I feel its strength,

magnificent and always surprising. The glorious rage rising up like hot mud, the familiar red coating my sight. It is useful in situations like these. Gretel taught me this.

"What the…" All he can say before I slam the bat into his gut, and he's soft like a sack of cotton. He goes down easy, kneeling on all his magazines, rolling over onto his mess.

I come closer and he snaps his head up to watch me, mind racing, trying to make sense of this. My mouth full of spit, the sweat is cascading down my back.

"You?" And he scrambles up, slipping on the glossy pages, stepping on all of their faces.

"How?" he keeps me in sight as he moves to the bed, onto and over, coming to the other side. Maybe he thinks he's safer there.

"Hello, Splint," I say and I can't help but smile. I walk closer to the bed, twisting the bat in my hands. I can't wait to get to him again, to see what damage I can do next.

"You're alive." He says in between fast gasps. "I thought they were rumors, the things I've heard."

He makes small talk to stall me. I come closer and I can smell his sweat, pungent with scare and disease. Strong enough to draw flies.

"Why don't you get the fuck outta here?"

I stop and stand motionless at the foot of the bed. I make myself still, command It to wait, savor the moment, tasting his fear that pours out of beady little eyes.

Then I see beady little eyes drop down to my thighs, just above the high, worn leather. I know *what he's looking for. I take away one hand from the bat, move it down to the scar, pressing on it, kneading it with my fingers. He watches my movements, the fear replaced by pathetic hunger. I can only imagine what he remembers, what visions he has dancing in his head.*

"It's here, right here," and I grab the flesh. "Would you like to touch it?"

For a split second he thinks about it, a faint smile coming to his sickly face. Then he looks up, and the want is extinguished.

"Is this good to you? Pleasing?" I move a little closer. "This mark you made, you like it?"

He says nothing, just stares and licks his lips.

I know his want because he wares it like a crown of thorns. I share this want too. I feel It pressing into my back, squeezing my throat. I know my anger has become complete, hot hate sliding into every thought, every movement. I welcome it's burn.

He moves towards me, cautiously. There's this look to him, self-assured, a growing confidence. "I heard some stories," his words oily, "that you were with Gretel for awhile. I could only imagine what happened to you there. I must have been a cake walk compared to what she did." Hyena mouth twisting upwards, he moves a little closer. "Do I still scare you, Lizard?"

In my dreams I have waited for this, this situation, these words. It's just like Christmas.

I raise the bat and slam it into his balls. He makes a high- pitched scream, and hits the floor with a force that almost knocks him out cold. I move fast, kneeling beside him, reaching down for white-blonde hair, feeling the greasy strands between my fingers. I jerk his head back, looking into blood shot eyes, searching for the weakness, finding it, watching the tears spilling silently into his gaping mouth. I should finish it. I should take what is mine. I have caused this suffering and I will cause more. But something's not right, there's something I should remember....

I will It to leave my head, pull out of my eyes. I feel its disgust as It retreats, sulking in the shadows of my mind. I must remember something. I close my eyes and light explodes, gold-tinged and warm. I see a little boy in the haze, crying and begging for someone to stop hurting him, stop burning him. I see Splint for who he is, the circles he follows, the patterns seared into his flesh. This

little boy, he hurt, was hurt, now makes the choice
to hurt back. Brother taught me this.

I fight back the rage, I try to calm myself down. I
have changed, I am different.

The stillness washes over me, and I release him,
sitting myself down on the stained sheets. I watch
him curl tighter into a ball, into himself.

"I didn't come here to kill you," I have to force
these words out, they taste treacherous, foreign.
"I've only come to give something back,
something of yours."

I get up, walk away from the bed and wait for
him to recover. Minutes go by, the slanting light
from the window growing golden, throwing long
shadows.

I watch his head poke up, the rest of him still
hiding behind the bed. "I think you should have

273

killed me when you had the chance," he says into the wadded up sheets, slowly standing with a knife in his hand, "I think you're gonna regret that you didn't, Leezard." He laughs, an ugly, unclean sound that makes my hair stand on end.

He rushes me, a stupid move. He's running fast but not fast enough. I step away, simple, an uncomplicated turn of my body, and he misses, slamming into the door. I raise the bat above my head, and know that this could be the last stroke. Let his death come here, now. I see the red cloud my sight, feel the stab in my shoulders.

He turns around quick and sees the bat coming down, and instead of bashing the side of his skull, I move it down, aiming for his cheek. A less lethal blow. He goes down in a fast twist, almost graceful in a way.

"Tricky bitch." He sneers up at me from a strange angle on the floor.

I kick him in the face. I feel his nose crunch against the side of my foot. He lands on his back at the side of the bed, trying to breathe through the blood.

I am calm. I can smell his blood. I am calm. I see it on my hand, on my foot, burns like wax. I am calm. I bring my hand to my mouth, tongue to the red spot, salty, metal taste spreading, sliding down my throat. I am calm. I have tasted him, I know him perfectly. Calm...calm.

I walk over to the bed and sit on the edge. His face is a mess of red bubbles. I reach down for his left arm, I pull it up tight, then slide my right leg down, stopping at his neck. I feel for the Adams apple, and go lower, applying pressure and most of my weight there with the ball of my foot. He

starts to choke, his other hand flying up to my leg,

ripping at my skin with dirty nails, doing damage

to my flesh. I flinch at the pain, move into it,

become it. Pure feeling that keeps me in the

moment, reminding me I am alive. I hold his other

hand tight as he thrashes, slowly suffocating.

"Like I said, I've come back to give you

something," the words dribble out and I try to

concentrate, bringing back the image of rough

solid, sharp heaviness. I go in between the moment

here and the moment inside. I dream with my eyes

open. Sugar taught me this.

He struggles underneath me, dying slowly.

Explosive coughing as I release my foot, his face

red with blood. I kneel down next to him, keeping

one hand on his throat.

I see it in my minds eye, I see it in a dream, the pain taking shape, the suffering made solid. I hold it in my hand, bring it out from my mind. I look down at Splint, still choking, and feel it against my fingers, heavy, clumsy, pain-filled. I feel it moving, trying to tell me everything, wanting me to relive and remember. I close my mind to its whispers and move it close to his heaving body, and I feel its want shifting, pulling towards him. I stay still, I go inside and picture his body opening up, like an incision at his stomach, yawning, growing wider. I plunge my hand inside, the rock giving it momentum, and I slide it in.

Splint screams beneath me, and there's warmth around my arm, a gentle sucking at my skin. Far away I can hear him crying, asking me to stop. I open my hand and release it, the hardness slipping away into his gut.

Something leaves me, an immeasurable weight dissipating, and I feel naked without it. I pull out my arm and see the blood on my skin.

"Six years I've carried that burden," the sound of my voice mixing with his wails, "and now I give it back."

I slowly rise, my legs shaky and weak.

"I forgive you, Splint." The sureness of my words startles me.

I leave him on the floor amongst the magazines and dirty clothes, twitching and bloody. Second task done, now to the third.

I walk down the hallway, counting my footsteps, feeling the cool wood underneath my feet. I come to a doorway, and I listen before going in.

"A final offer, Riggs. Come to this family, leave that old hag and work for us."

"Work for who, fat man? Your family grows smaller with each passing year, I wonder why that is?" Riggs voice sounding dangerous, he is always so protective of Sugar.

I walk into the room and see Razor standing in front of the desk, arms behind his back, composed and perfect. His jaw is tight, the green restrained behind slits that focused on the huge bloated thing in front of him. My eyes catch Johnston's glance and he looks confused.

"What surprises," a frown etched into his sweating face, "another one back from the dead." Mopping his forehead, thinking of a way to get control of the situation. " A day of reunions! Truly, a day to celebrate!"

He tries to smile but his fear of ghosts betray him.

I hear Riggs behind me, the click of a lighter, flash of a flame, a puff of smoke and he clears his throat, "Gila. Prophet of Sugar. Didn't you know this, Johnston?"

Johnston's eyes light up, going greedy. "So it is true? She's the one? Dreams the things to come?" He shifts heavy in the white chair. "I have heard, yes, but I thought they were just stories." He looks at me with new interest.

"So is it true, girl? What they say?"

I hear the screaming of the cook's wife inside my head, see the spreading blood underneath the cook that leaks out from his opened throat, bound and gagged on the kitchen floor.

"A proposition. Money and immunity if you will come to the fold. Come dream for me." Swollen hand tapping at his barreled chest as his words slither out into the open space between us.

"Sounds too good to be true," I say, looking over at Razor, playing the game.

He watches me carefully before choosing his response. *"Razor has decided to come back and I just know that you would make a fine addition to this family. Let's call it a reunion, shall we?"* And he smiles, greasy jowls shiver with the charade.

I'm looking at the whiteness of the walls, the ugly shine of the desk.

"But I'm sure you want closure."

I stare at the shelves with nothing on them, serving no purpose.

" I will send for Splint, to give his apologies of course."

White all around me, everywhere, and I close my eyes for the comfort of the blackness.

"Don't bother," I say. "It's all just water under the bridge," and I open my eyes, grab the back of a white chair and smear it with red, smiling at the mess I made.

If I close my eyes, I can see her. If I let my hand fall on the notebook in front of me, it starts to write, automatic and unnatural. I'm scared. What do I do after something like this? I can still hear her voice if I listen, thick and whispery rich.

I can feel it lodged in my throat like some kind of parasite, waiting, biding its time.

I don't even want to start thinking about Hailey.

I can still smell her on my skin, like fresh cotton,

like crushed grass.

I'm so tired. Burned out beyond belief.

Hallucinations? Everything I saw was something

I wanted to see, something already pre-made and

waiting to happen. This is a little more comforting

than the thought that I relived these details, a

reality of epic mementos filled with pain and

suffering. Or maybe I'm going insane.

One more thing I should add before I go get

drunk.

The last vision, the one where Gila sees the

vision of Johnston's cook, well I saw this one too.

When she pictured him on the tiled floor, throat

slit, drowning in his own blood, I saw this too. I

recognized his face. I have that face. My father's

face. Why did she dream about my father? Reason says that it might have been my own dreams coming through, mingling in. It was towards the end, I guess. But that voice doesn't sound so convincing these days.

Only one thing to do, go there tomorrow, run up those stairs, open that door, go straight in, see her there chained to the bed, and politely ask her if this is real. All of it.

And if it is?

June 25, Friday, 11:23 PM

It seems like a million years ago when I woke up
Thursday afternoon after a shitty eight hour nap of
tossing and screaming. I got dressed and left for
the house. I couldn't wait any longer.

The place seemed empty when I got there, the
lengthening light of the afternoon deepening the
shadows behind every corner, spreading like
spidery fingers from underneath all the doors. I
walked up the stairs, muscles groaning with each
step. I prepared myself for the change, feeling the
heat turning a little more dry and light, taking
away my sweat, leading me closer.

My head was throbbing, aftershocks from the
surreal experiences of the previous night. I didn't
feel well, I wasn't myself, and my head was still

buzzing with all the questions, heavy with the visions.

I moved past Johnston's office, closed and silent. I stopped to take off my shoes, to feel the cool wood under my feet as I walked, counting the footsteps. I stopped at Splint's door and looked down at the knob, knowing what happened inside, knowing him without knowing. Knowing I hate him. Did I want to go in?

Almost.

I made my way to the end of the hallway, to the thin flight of fragile stairs. I could feel my heart skip and my hands sweat. Images of her filled my mind, and I tried so hard to push them away, so afraid of what I would see. But deep down I wanted them to blind me. Deep down I still feel the sting of her pleas, wanting them, wanting her.

The dryness of the heat was intensifying as I climbed. My legs shook as bad as the stairs. Almost there, I could see the matchstick railing, see the closed door.

I focused on that door and went to it grabbing the knob. My mind snapped shut at the thought of her behind it as my actions were put on automatic. Sweat coated the glass in my hand, and I twisted it barely, gently and the squeak of the hinge brought me back to the tension and anticipation. Would she be there?

The faint light from the hallway below hardly let me see what was in the room. But I knew. I could smell her, the way the heat was sweet, the thin scent of flowers covered in sand. My mouth watered.

My eyes adjusted to the dusk. My chest tightened.

There, on the end of the bed she sat. Shadowy she starred back, calm, untouched, expecting me.

"Gila?" I could hardly say it. I felt my legs going to water, my knees wanting the floor.

Then she spoke, her voice matching the echoes in my head. "Charlie," she whispered just for me, knowing my name without me telling. "Open the blinds for me," the sound snapping my knees into place as I moved to the small window, the only window, and twisted the wood rod, letting the amber soaked light into the room.

I turned around.

She was still there, sitting on the small bed, face turned towards the light, bathed in gold. She was real. She was here.

In my mind a thousand images snaked past, showing me all the things, letting me see everything again. Do I question it? Call them hallucinations?

I opened my eyes, stinging with sweat, to her face, to her eyes. She had come to the other side of the bed, and I could see those long legs draped over the side. Skin smooth and bronzed, and I moved my eyes up, looking for the scar. Following the thin chain around her ankle, sliding up her right thigh, tight and long, curving towards the inside. Her legs were moving, opening up, and then I saw it, the pale dip in her flesh, the ragged oval carved into the skin.

I slid to my knees, my sight still stuck on the scar as I rearranged the evidence in my head.

"Surrender to it, Charlie," her voice coated me in hot honey. I slowly looked up to see her smiling down, dark and dangerous, and suddenly she was something to be wary of, something to fear. But it didn't matter, I was hers, I had been for a long time already. Still am.

Then her head turned towards the door, listening, smile fading.

"He's coming."

I disconnected from her face and looked to the door. Who?

"Into the wardrobe, quick. Quiet." She looked back at me, finger to her lips.

I scrambled up, feet sticky with panic, I made my way to the wardrobe, opened it and stuffed myself in. Muffled silence surrounded me in the form of old coats and blankets. I closed the door most of the way, leaving a space so I could see

and hopefully hear as well. A space that always

seemed to get me in trouble.

I could see her turn away from the wardrobe to

the door, staring at it, willing it to open. She sat on

the edge of the bed, or it could have been a cliff,

waiting for the storm to move in, watching the

huge bloated clouds condensing, feeling the air

change, the threat becoming substantial and

palatable. The door opened, the clouds parted, and

the great white hurricane stood before her.

"Gila, you're awake. Wonderful!" Thunder in

the words, sinister and hidden in the gloom of his

voice.

He carried a glass of water in a puffy hand,

"Here, you look thirsty."

She didn't move.

He shrugged and brought it to his fat face, draining it with a gulp. He licked his lips and smiled. "The prophecies have been true, job well done." He waddled over to the open blinds, looking out.

I heard the rattle of the chain against the bed's metal frame. He turned back around. "But I'm not letting you go yet."

Her eyes stalked him, watching his every move. " I thought we had an agreement." She softly said.

Johnston snorted, turning away. "Oh yes, that. Well there's good reason for our actions, that's all you need to know." Coming back around to stand in front of her. "In fact, I have a new proposal." Grabbed a chair, slid it to the front of the bed. Carefully he lowered his gigantic ass onto it and took out his handkerchief. "Let me just say that your service to the family has been… almost loyal," and wiped his gleaming forehead. "But you see, it's Razor. He's always been such a great asset to our family, so valuable, well, until you came. Now he's disobedient, unpredictable."

"Will you ever get to the point, Pig?" Her voice surprised me.

"Temper, temper. There's no need for that tone with me." Johnston said dangerously, anger danced in his small eyes. "Consider yourself lucky, after this I'm letting both of you go. Your family obligations will be over."

I heard her laugh softly, shaking her head. "Letting go meaning putting bullets in our heads? Isn't that what you meant to say, Pig?"

"Quit calling me that!" He roared, his face going beet red. He leaned over in his chair, bringing himself closer to her. "Shut your mouth and listen to me because there's one more thing you will do. I know you can dream deaths, the way a person might go out." Sweat cascaded into his eyes, over the thick rolls of skin. "Dream my death and I'll let you go. Do it. Or both of you will die."

He brought the now dripping handkerchief to meet the wet mess of his face, but instead it slipped out of his sausaged mitt, onto the floor. I watched him bend down, waiting for that suit to split open but instead something better happened.

Touching it with his hand, he almost had it, but he didn't realize how close he had gotten to the bed.

She moved so fast.

He fell to the floor with a crash, his legs kicked out from underneath him. With a viciousness that shocked me, she reached his neck, grabbed it, and dragged him towards her. How could she have handled all that weight? Then I thought of the separate part, the strength that always surprised her and felt my adrenaline sucker punch me.

He was on his knees, head wrenched back sharply, spine bent painfully, arching the floor. Her hands around the thick of his throat, muscles shivered under her skin. Her eyes were dark and she smiled, enjoying this as I watched her through the secret space of the door. I watched her move, watched how the anger flowed smooth around her like water, her violence shimmered like hot sunshine over those dark eyes. I couldn't look away, even though a part of me was afraid of what I might see. That maybe I would see *It*.

"Now, Pig, you will listen," her voice different, distorted. My eyes snapped away to focus on the dark fur of a coat.

"Quit moving or I'll slit your throat right here, and then we all can dine on swine tonight." She hissed and then laughed low and gritty.

Through the late afternoon sun I could see the gold of the light behind her turn darker, slowly staining red.

"I'll dream your death."

My chest hurt with the fear, throat closing, couldn't breathe.

"No morphine, no visitors."

His face was turning purple.

"Tomorrow at noon, Slather's warehouse. You'll get what you need."

I couldn't stand the closeness of the space any longer. I closed my eyes to calm myself down. But I wanted to see *It*. Just a glimpse.

She stood up from the bed, bringing him with her, forcing him to his feet. I searched her shoulders, her back, the top of her head. Was there something there? Something clinging to her neck, buried in her skull?

With a strangled grunt, she heaved him towards the door, and I heard him slam into the railing, splintered sounds echoing down the hallway, then heavy footfalls down the stairs, hurried and panicked. He was gone.

I fell out of the cabinet, engorging my lungs with fresh air, and looked over at Gila. She sat there looking back at me like nothing had ever happened. She smiled.

This time it was sweet and young. No darkness, only sun and a slight shade of sadness. I found myself crawling across the floor, drawn to that shine, to her.

"Do you know why you're here, Charlie?" Words soft, rimmed with faint pain.

Did I know why I was here? I looked up into her eyes, hazel infused with shards of green and silky threads of rust. "To ask you something," I barely managed to say.

She blinked, releasing me, and I found myself very close to her. She smiled again, and looked down at her arm. I did too, and saw that the inside of her elbow was bruised a muddy purple and it made me sad. She touched it, pushed down on it, and fresh blood seeped up from the place that Johnston slid his needle into.

"Do you know why you are here?" Said again, just as soft. She brought her eyes up again to mine, looking deep into them, reaching into my head. I was here with her, just me. No one else.

"No."

"I think you do," and the color of her irises turned deeper, swirling, changing. I could feel the heat of the room soak into me, swallowing me whole. I stared harder, watched as her pupils dilated, opening wide like flowers, and there I saw a light, a pinhole of sun. I felt myself following it, like running down a tunnel. Faster, faster, finally catching it, and it flooded my mind with intense light, blinding and confusing me.

Where am I? I tried to say it, but the words weren't there.

I heard something behind me like small laughter, and then I was back in her eyes, surrounded by the color that was turning from hazel to a warm gold.

And this is where I saw the sun.

I stood in a desert, a gold-lavender landscape in the midst of twilight. Around me, a thousand pale lilies slowly nodding, closing their eyes to a falling sun, the heat intense even though the sun was setting.

My lungs sucked deep into the hot air, head felt light, disconnected. Then something behind me again, but when I spun around nothing was there. Whatever it was, it still lingered. I could sense it surrounding me with great tenacious arms, huge and heavy.

I could see something forming out of the hills of sand, realizing it was her eyes. The gold in them was blinding if I stared at them too long, so I looked back to the flowers, watching the petals closing, slowly wilting.

I was dripping with the heat. I was melting into this landscape, just like the lilies. I was in two places at once and I felt like I couldn't hold on, but she held me fast between the desert and the gold of her eyes. I could feel my head expanding, the space between my eyes growing, taking up weight.

Then I noticed the sand turning colors, like blood running over the soft hills. No, not the sand, her lips, there was blood on her lips.

My eyes were closing, too heavy with the heat and visions. I felt like I slipping away. 'Too much,' I thought to myself, 'give me release,' and the desert seemed to hear the request, because it sent a cool wind slithering along the low hills and flowers, wrapping around me, wiping away the heat and wet from my clammy skin.

Why was I here?

Because my mother is dead. Please let her know I'm here.

My thoughts were on the edge of delirium, and nothing was making sense. Then the desert started to change, became heavy. The air itself seemed to collapse around me, pushing me down to the sand. I grabbed it in my hands, the grains pushing through my fingers, hot and gritty, turning smooth and wet.

Then at that moment everything turned red. A thick, luscious color, saturated with hunger and anger. Through the compressed heat I could see her lips, soft and open, smeared with the blood. I needed to touch them, hold them in my mouth. I

was so thirsty.

Why am I here?

I crawled through the bleeding sand and I could

hear the thought again in my head. My mother.

My father. This is why I am here.

Why?

Why are you dead? What did I do for you to

leave me? Mom, what did I do? Why did you send

me away?

I was closer now and I could feel her breath

touch my face, the breeze of the desert, salty-hot

on my skin.

Dad, where the hell are you? Why did you

leave? Are you dead too because I can feel it. Why

else wouldn't you come to her funeral?

I hurt so bad, the emotion as heavy as the air, crushing me, suffocating me.

What do I know? I feel the question come into my mind like a moth, fluttering close to the warmth of the memories. What do I know? Don't know, just want. Coming closer to the red of her lips, closer to oblivion.

I felt my hands touch something firm, solid, and warm. The sand below me was changing, the air lifting, the vision wiping away to the sight of her face so close to mine. My hands were on her knees, spreading them apart to move in between, to feel her lips, taste them, lick the blood away like water.

Like water, yes and I pressed my mouth over hers, hard, hungry, so incredibly thirsty. She felt softer, different than what I had imagined. The moment fragile, unstable, ripening into its prime, verge of decay. I took her lips into my mouth, sucking away the blood, wanting nothing more than this. I felt her tongue slither out, touching mine, sensation electric, addicting. Then she was pulling away, the inevitable was happening, the apple falling from the tree.

I teetered on my sore knees, swaying, as the whole room spun. I could taste metal, rusty iron under my tongue. I swallowed thick blood, feeling it hit my stomach, coiling into something angry. My head was opening up, a feeling of weightlessness overtook me and I couldn't feel the floor anymore. But this was all happening way too fast, and my heart skipped to herald the arrival of panic. Suddenly the sands were starting to disappear, her sun-tinged eyes were turning darker, and the hardness of the wood under my knees seemed to return.

I opened my eyes to the real world. I could see her sitting on the bed, the faint smile on her face saying nothing had really happened.

But my head felt different, the space behind my eyes tingled and burned. Deep inside my skull that place itched and twitched. I knew better than to believe her smile.

The room was getting hazy. It was getting really hot but I started to shiver, getting colder. I wanted to be warm and lost in those eyes again. No, needed to. I started to get up but the room was swimming and I fell to the ground.

"The blood speaks to you," the warmth in her words gave me the heat I needed and I stopped shivering for a second. "Fever dreams are coming.

Go now and remember, Charlie," her voice ricocheting inside my sore head.

I didn't want to go. Don't make me go. I felt so lost and cold, the chills sinking deeper into my skin. I tried again to get up, knees like rubber, muscles liquefied. Finally I found myself standing, making my way back to Gila.

She was staring at me, into me. "No," her voice was heavy, thicker. I remembered this, the anger coming. I looked behind her because something was happening, something staining the air pink. I didn't think I wanted to see this.

I fell again so I started to crawl. I slowly reached the hallway, my knees aching, skin crawling, hot then cold. The hall was full of shadows. Hungry, evil shades that wanted to hurt me and swallow me whole.

I had to get out. I had to go home.

I heard footsteps behind me but I couldn't move.
I tried to turn my head to the sound but all I saw
was blackness and a humid heat touched my face.
A hand seemed to materialize from the smear of
shadow and reached down for me.

Razor's face was heavy with his usual concern
as he pulled me up from the ground. I stood there
wobbling on useless legs, amazed that he was
there. I watched him go into Gila's room. I
watched her face as she saw him, so happy to see
him, so happy.

I wanted to go back in. I was remembering all
the questions I needed to ask, all the things I
wanted to say. But my head started to throb and
the room started to spin.

When I looked back at them, I could see that Razor was on his knees, Gila embracing him, holding him in her arms. He would have her warmth now, not me. I watched her hand slide through his dark hair, fingers slowly pulling his head back. Razor's smooth neck arched, his face tense, muscles knotted between his eyes. He seemed in pain, but there was a faint smile on his lips.

Reason screamed that I shouldn't be watching this, that I should go, leave this place forever.

I watched Gila bring her face close to his, kissing his cheeks lightly, barely. Then Razor opened his eyes, the green intense and watery, and he looked up, letting streams of huge tears run over his pale face.

Why was he crying?

'Maybe not crying,' something whispered from the shadows, 'maybe releasing, letting go, and giving back.' I searched the hateful stains of black that hung around me on the stairwell and could see nothing to make this observation. Now I was hearing things.

Gila was catching the tears with her mouth, her lips, lips that were just touching mine. She slowly licked, lapping up the salty wetness from his face.

I needed to go.

But I couldn't move. Something was coming into view, something hunching the curve of her back, something clutching the broadness of her shoulders. I stared as hard as I could, trying to define it, see it more clearly.

It piggy- backed her, riding her shoulders like a demonic playmate. I could see the mottled scales, the soft smear of drying blood. But I couldn't see the face, because It was wearing her like a mask, seeing through her, licking away the salt from Razor's face. From it's own lost eyes.

I knew it was time to go even though it was hard to look away. My ears started to ring, head spinning, my body falling apart. I looked down the stairs and wondered how I was ever going to get down them.

Then I felt something on my back, a steady pressure, and I turned to see if it was Razor again, but no one was there. I started the descent so slowly, the phantom arm at my back when I started to spin, when I was sure I wouldn't make it.

When I got to the front door, I had almost forgotten where I was, everything so thick and dream-like slow. Outside the sun was going down in flames, the orange glow intense, almost overwhelming to my fevered brain. I watched as the dark surrounded the sinking sun, how the light gave away to the black, melding the two together in some other- worldly marriage. I understood suddenly that they were not opposite of each other but that they were *other*, different aspects of the same thing. Was I making sense? Were these thoughts coherent?

I stumbled to my car, the gravel growling under my bare feet, the sharpness of the rocks biting into my soles. I finally made it, and I opened the door, the rushing heat welcome to my shivering skin. I crawled inside and curled up into the fading warmth of cracked vinyl.

I woke up to the sound of a car starting up and driving away. When I moved my head it felt broken, my neck stiff and brittle. Outside it was pitch black, I wondered what time it was. My brain was throbbing, mouth dry and glued shut at the edges. I needed water.

When I got out of the car my legs seemed to be better, at least I could stand without falling on my ass. I made my way back to the house, but decided that it wouldn't be a good idea going in through the front door. I still wasn't supposed to be here after dark. Instead I would sneak in.

The kitchen window was open a crack, so I got a garbage can and dragged it over. My muscles hurt, my skin hurt, bones, and all major organs. I was so fucking thirsty.

I stood on the lid and opened the window, crawled over and landed with a clumsy thump on the other side. I stood in the dark for a second just to make sure no one was close by.

Nothing.

I walked to the sink.

All of a sudden it was bright, I thought I was busted, someone turning on the lights to see what all the noise was about. But this was a different light, more clear. I looked to my right and saw my father standing there at the sink, peeling potatoes, sunlight pouring in through the window.

Then he was gone.

I started to panic. Jesus, I was tripping balls. What the fuck did she do to me? Don't think about what you just saw. Get to the sink, get the water.

The kitchen gleamed in the semi-darkness. Yes, darkness, not daylight. I cranked open the faucet and bent underneath it, drinking deep, gulping fast. It felt so good rushing down my shriveled throat, until it hit my stomach. The water was too cold and my fever too hot, and it came back up as fast as I put it down.

I heard shouting. It was familiar, my stomach quivered with the sound.

The lights came on and I saw Splint and Slather drag my mother across the kitchen floor. She was screaming, my father's voice in the background, yelling, angry. Then I saw him next to me, on the floor, bound up and hog tied, laying on his side.

I went to move, not knowing what to do first, when they all faded and disappeared. My heart pounded, spots bloomed in front of my eyes. I was convinced I was dying.

The room seemed to get darker after that hallucination, going even darker as I looked around. I started to see things moving in the thick shadows, swirling, slithering.

I was shaking so bad that I fell to my knees, hands on the cool tile, on reality, something solid.

And then something hissed close to my face.

I closed my eyes, waiting for the illusion to fade just like the others. But when I opened them, the kitchen was bathed in a bizarre glow. I looked around to see where the light was coming from this time, unbelieving of the greenish-golden haze. Then I saw the walls, they were the source, wait…not the walls. Something was moving, like a stream, a river of phosphorescent motion over the walls themselves.

Lizards.

They poured from the walls, ran over onto the floor, flowing across the tile. The swarm made its way to me, but they didn't stop. They crawled over my hands, onto my arms, burning me as they ran, making me shiver even harder than before.

Hundreds? Thousands? This was insane. I opened my mouth to laugh as loud as I could, to let them all know I got the joke, and that's when they poured past my lips. They tasted salty and warm as they ran over my tongue, straining against my cheeks. Then I could feel my mouth moving without my permission, my lips forming the words, the sound of lizards speaking through me, "Give you dreaming," the noise of buzzing drones drowning in quicksand.

That was it. I was done for.

I stood up, lizards clinging to my legs, my face, running over my feet as I moved, as I stumbled again to find something solid, something real.

So dizzy and sick, coughing back reptiles that tried to pour down my throat.

I made it to the stove and put my hands on the cool enamel to steady myself. Something vibrated through the steel into my spread palms, something deep and hot. Then from the burners, huge orange flames shot straight up into the air, right past my face as I tried to jump back, but my hands seemed stuck in place, and all I could do was scream at the heat. As I stared into the flames, I could see something inside moving back and forth,

something with huge eyes, gold and sun-tinged.

There was another lizard deep in the heat, but this

one was a monster and he was looking straight at

me. I needed to touch it, test it, to see if the fire

was real. If any of this was real.

I picked up my hand, unstuck from the stove,

and plunged it into the flames.

"Do you know why you are here, Charlie?"

Her voice clear as soon as I touched its burning

scales.

The kitchen lit up again. Oh, God, not again.

I looked towards the sink to see my father at the

floor, sliding down in the thickening puddle of his

blood that poured from his flayed throat.

Johnston was bent over the butcher block island

in the middle of the room, bent over something,

no, someone. My mother's face twisted with loathing, her mouth bound with tight cloth.

Then all around me, the jarring sound of pigs squealing and screaming.

I felt the slime of mud between my toes as the rain splashed into huge puddles. The raw stench of pig shit, the low sound of thunder. He was all over in this huge field of muck, all in pieces around me. I could see the bloated forms of swine as they rooted around, looking for all the tasty tidbits that had been cut up and scattered for them to devour. My father all around in pieces, my brain hurt with the thought of this.

Something touched my arm, then pressure around my fingers, warm and steady. I looked up to see him, all in one piece, holding my hand, leading me out of the mud.

Then gone.

Tears choking my eyes, pain in every movement I made.

I was back in our house, where it was warm and the light was so familiar. I looked down to see Splint writing on a piece of paper on our kitchen table, long, cursive letters, signing my father's name. I see her heaped upon the small writing desk, her thin wrists leaking red color all over his forged note.

Before the anger could set in, before the thought had time to realize, I smelled something sweet. Arms coming around me, pressure on my shoulders. I looked back to see her brown eyes looking into mine.

Then my mom was gone. Faded away into nothing.

Too much to feel and too many pigs screaming, I couldn't hold on any longer.

I woke up in the kitchen with real daylight streaming through the window. Stiff and achy, I sat up, looked around. I remembered all the visions, everything that had happened, everything came crashing back, loud and painful. What did she do to me?

The blood, something in it, had to be but what? Then the realization of it all, the cold shock setting in.

Johnston killed my parents.

My stomach started to heave.

Gila dreamt that it would happen then they tried to kill her.

My hands shook uncontrollably.

Because my parents wouldn't do what the fat fuck wanted, they died. Fed my dad to the pigs and slit my mom's wrists.

One final heave of my stomach and puke was everywhere on the floor. There was blood in it.

Why was this happening?

"What happened to you?"

I turned to the dirty, hoarse voice, to Splint standing in the doorway.

"Hey, what's with the gloomy mug, Chuck?"

Just the sound of his voice put me over the edge. My hate condensed into something pointed and ugly and I aimed it right at him, without me really knowing what was happening.

"How's the stomach, fucker?"

Splint just stood there, a confused look on his face, as I tried to figure out why I just asked him that.

"What did you say?"

"Your stomach? You know, the cancer. Is it spreading?" My words bringing something to his eyes, "You remember don't you, Splint? The gift she gave back to you?"

He walked up to me, "What do you know about that?" His voice quiet, I think I struck a nerve.

"You know you're lucky she let you live." I was amazed at my words.

He rushed down to me, his face pure fury as he pulled me up. "You don't know anything! She's a goddamned devil whore and she should have died on that fucking road right where I left her!" I could smell the stench of rotten beer vapors and the sour of old cigarettes on his breath.

"So it's true? You can't get it up so good these days? Maybe it's the cancer that's doing it to you or maybe the guilt...." Not my words, but I really didn't mind.

But then, right before my eyes he turned into that mass of evil that I had seen so many times through Gila.

"Oh, I can get it up, don't worry about that, Charlie Boy. In fact," pulling out something fast from behind him, a sharp click in my ear, "I'll show you.'

With a gun to my head, he shoved me through the kitchen door, down the hall, and up the stairs.

"In there, asshole," shoving me into the tiny bathroom on the second floor. I tried not to think about what he wanted to do. I felt the gun move away from my ear and I turned around. He stood there unzipping his pants, gun held tight in the other hand.

Oh hell no.

"Fuck this," my voice loud in the small space, he looked at me and hesitated, just for a second. Maybe he wouldn't do this.

"No," then the look was gone. "No, fuck you, little boy." He came closer, hand fumbling inside his jeans. Without thinking, I tackled him into the bathtub, his head bashing into the faucet. He recovered quickly and spun around to face me.

"That's it, fucker!" Splint screamed and shoved the gun into my face. I slowly rose out of the tub and stood there watching him scramble to his feet, blood dripping down his cheek. He stepped over the side and swung his arm, his fist connecting

with my nose. I spun and landed face down next to

the toilet. I could feel the barrel of the gun dig into

my temple as he started to rip off my pants.

He wasn't doing this. Right? Raped and killed

like my mother. Raped and damaged like Gila, and

I flashed back to her eyes, gold and sun-tinged.

Yes, her eyes. Think of something else while he

did this.

My hands snaked around the porcelain of the

toilet, focusing on its cool wetness, thankful of it.

Then I felt something brush my finger, something

quick and warm, crawling into my open hand. I

remembered the lizards then, how hot they felt as

they swarmed over me in the kitchen.

Then the gun disconnected from my head and I felt his other hand help out with my forced disrobing.

This was it. Whatever was in my fist would help me because I already knew what it was and I knew it would let me escape the impending doom of his disease.

I flipped over and flung the thing into his startled face. I heard myself laughing as I watched the lizard stick to his cheek like a piece of barbed wire. Splint screamed and clawed at it like it was searing his skin. He jumped up and headed for the sink, dropping his gun. I slid over and grabbed it. When I came up behind him, I looked into the mirror and saw his panicked face, but no lizard.

I lined the gun up with his head, thought about what I was about to do, judged that he had this coming, no, he had much worse coming but I only had that moment to rectify what he had done and I squeezed the trigger.

Nothing.

The mother had conned me with an empty piece.

Well, I decided I had to do something, so I raised the gun high above my head and brought it down on his skull. He swayed a little before he dropped to his knees, bashing his chin on the sink before he cleared the floor.

Did I kill him? Don't know, all I did know was that a meeting was happening soon, at Slather's warehouse, if I didn't miss it already. Something told me to hurry.

I ran down the stairs, out of the house, into the car. As I drove, I replayed all the images, all the sounds. The loudest were the screams of my mother.

Electric blue loomed in front of me, the beginning of this whole mess. I stopped the car on the street, ran the rest of the way. I turned the corner and saw a small crowd in the parking lot. I slammed to a halt and looked around. I spotted some bushes growing at the edge of the pavement where everybody stood. I took the scenic route through a weedy field until I came to the spot and hid in the green cool of the shrubs, waiting.

Then I saw him. The core of it all, wasn't he? I think I hated him even more than Splint. He was the one who took both of them away from me.

I could hear her cries coming from all around. My head was pounding, my heart slamming and my mom wouldn't stop screaming.

I will make him sorry.

My thoughts were turning a dark shade of violent, becoming jagged, raw.

I would kill him. I would kill him and watch him bleed into the ground and then I will tell him who I am and he will scream and cry and beg and I will watch him bleed and die and die and he will be so sorry.

I edged closer to the crowd. I was so close but they didn't know how close I was.

And there she was.

She was standing there with Razor, the harsh sun beating down on them, the light coloring her skin a luscious bronzed sheen. Worn leather shorts rode high on her curved thighs and her legs were so long. Her feet were bare.

Razor stood there close to her, protective. His pale skin was sweaty, his black clothes pressed and perfect. His face was a mirror of concentration, his brows knitted with intense concern and those eyes burning that impossible green.

There were two other men with the pig and they stood slightly behind him on each side. One was Slather's guy, fat and stupid. The other one was Simms and he looked sick and greasy. I knew why they were there. No one was leaving this family alive.

There was something heavy in my hands…

I knew why he wanted this, why he wanted to know his death. To be ready for it, to cheat it, live to molest another day.

Johnston spoke first, "Let's get this over with."

As soon as he spoke, Slather's gorilla passed out behind him, hitting the ground with a thud. Johnston turned around to see the sound and shook his head, reached inside his white coat and pulled out a gun.

"Let's proceed, shall we?" And pointed it at Gila and Razor.

Gila slipped a glance towards Razor, slight smile on her lips. She turned to Johnston, stepping up to meet him face to face.

"You have asked me to dream your death. So be it," her voice steady and low. "I have seen your way as well as your life, both wasted and soiled. I have also seen your death and she was weeping."

This seemed to hit him in a weird way. He twitched, a look of uncertainty washed over his bloated face.

"Your death will come in the eyes of one you have missed. Left behind in the trail of shit that has always followed you." The look in her eyes became hard and gleaming.

My head exploded with the blinding visions of my mom's terrified face. They made her watch as they dismembered my father. This couldn't go on anymore. It wouldn't. I started to lurch from the bushes, something still heavy in my hand. I could hear Gila's voice like it was a million miles away.

"The forgotten has returned and the occasion is remembered."

I walked behind Simms, hit him over the head and he went down just like Splint. So easy.

"Turn around, Pig. Meet your death."

Her words are like honey, I thought to myself. They melt in the sun soaked heat.

I was right behind him now, could smell the tang of rancid sweat hiding in white fabric. He turned around so slowly and when his eyes met mine, I couldn't think. All I could hear was the sound of my mother screaming. I didn't even hear the firing of the gun I held in my hand. A gun that should have been empty.

He fell heavy to the blacktop, his blood way too red, devouring the white cotton of his suit and then, well he was dead. I couldn't even tell him who I really was, what that cook was to me, the woman he killed, how I avenged them and how he lost.

I looked up and saw her staring at me. I found those eyes and couldn't look away. I wanted to drown myself in her heavy desert. I wanted to die right there.

Then it all went black.

I woke up in my hotel room, all my stuff gone except for a pack of Marlboro reds, a lighter and my journal. My car is still parked at the warehouse so I'm not sure who brought me back although I do have a feeling that it was Gila and Razor. What I do know for sure is that there has been someone standing outside my door for the past hour or so. I can hear small quiet noises, tiny whispers, shuffling of feet. I don't want to open it, can't be sure it isn't someone from the family waiting to bash my head in for what I did to the fat fuck.

Anyway I started writing as soon as consciousness set in. I couldn't stop, automatic like before, manic and rabid.

When I close my eyes, I see her sun tinged ones looking back. She knew everything, brought me here, got inside my head. I know we both were bound with that same agony, both drowning in the same black water. Her head was just a little higher than mine so she could see the land when all I could see was the despair of a cold, bottomless ocean. She ran me in a maze of mirrors and fire, warmed me up and let me see who I could be, what I could do.

She put the gun in my hand and I pulled the trigger.

So what next? Jump out the window? Call the cops? Invite them in for fucking tea? I don't even know who is out there or what they want.

(Maybe they're waiting for me to wrap this up.)

Our hero reluctantly puts down his pen and slowly gets up from the small dingy bed that he has been sitting on for the past several hours.

Finally making up his mind on what to do, he moves towards the door, and with great intent, grabs the knob....

Wish me luck.

.